Praise

"...Stacey May Fowles... is a writer filled with talent and insight... The writing is sharp and evocative and shows a deep level of sympathy for the characters and keen psychological understanding."
Broken Pencil Magazine

"...Stacey May Fowles demonstrates a budding mastery over the poetic aspects of prose. She showers the reader time and again with rhythmically beautiful sentences... Her skill in using unique description to create evocative landscapes and mindscapes has a hypnotic effect... enchanting..."
The Feminist Review

"...voices that feel bracingly honest, fresh and jaded in the same breath."
The Globe and Mail

FEAR OF FIGHTING

Fear of Fighting

Words by Stacey May Fowles
Pictures by Marlena Zuber

Invisible Publishing
Halifax & Montréal

Library and Archives Canada Cataloguing in Publication

Fowles, Stacey May
    Fear of fighting / written by Stacey May Fowles ; illustrated by
Marlena Zuber.
ISBN 978-0-9782185-5-3
    I. Zuber, Marlena II. Title.
PN6733.F69F42 2008   741.5'971   C2008-905712-0

Designed by Megan Fildes
Cover and interior illustration by Marlena Zuber

Typeset in Laurentian by Megan Fildes
With thanks to type designer Rod McDonald

Questions on page 81 borrowed from *Pregnant, Now What?*—www.plannedparenthood.org

Printed and bound in Canada

Invisible Publishing
Halifax & Montréal
www.invisiblepublishing.com

Fear of Fighting was produced with the support of the Canada Council for the Arts, the
Ontario Arts Council, and the City of Toronto through the Toronto Arts Council.

We acknowledge the support of the Canada Council for the Arts which last year invested
$20.1 million in writing and publishing throughout Canada.

Invisible Publishing recognizes the support of the Province of Nova Scotia through the
Department of Tourism, Culture & Heritage. We are pleased to work in partnership with
the Culture Division to develop and promote our cultural resources for all Nova Scotians.

NOVA SCOTIA
Tourism, Culture and Heritage

Canada Council   Conseil des Arts
for the Arts   du Canada

ONTARIO ARTS COUNCIL
CONSEIL DES ARTS DE L'ONTARIO

torontoartscouncil
An arm's length body of the City of Toronto

For Spencer, who always helps me find the exits.

PROLOGUE

There are lots of songs that have been written about girls. Thousands of millions of songs about girls. Wicked women and sidewalk stomping vixens. Daddy's little girls and preacher's daughters. Sweet, doe-eyed babies and bitchy, addictive heroines.

Sometimes I think of Marnie as all of those clichéd tunes mashed up. Every time I hear one of them over the loud speaker in the No Frills, while carefully deciding between frozen peas and peaches-and-cream corn, I can only think about her. I think about her living across the hall from me. Her cluttered apartment packed with relics, her rescue cat and her tiny, paint-peeling kitchenette. I think about how the walls are so paper-thin that I can occasionally hear her singing in the shower.

I wish she was mine.

I can't have her though. She's someone else's. Someone else who clearly has no idea what they have.

Marnie across the hall doesn't know I love her and her clutter and her singing and how the idea of having her keeps me sane. And Marnie will likely never know any of this.

Marnie doesn't know that anyone loves her. Marnie doesn't even know that she is lovable.

Some days I run into her in the hallway and she tries to smile at me, but it's clear she doesn't have much to smile about.

"Here," she seems to say, with her sad, awkward stance, "I dare you to try to unbreak what's been broken."

I would know what I had if I had Marnie.

THERE ARE SONGS ABOUT GIRLS........

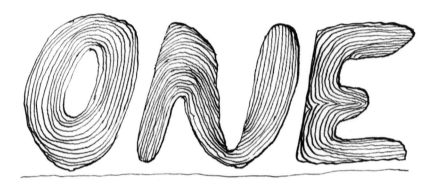

ONE

Tracey, the local tomboy who lived down the street from me, taught me how to kiss boys when I was eleven years old.

Tracey knew more about boys than I did simply because she had an older brother and I did not. She knew what boys smelled like, what they liked to eat, how and when they did their laundry, and how long it took them to shave. Because of this I trusted her when she told me what they liked and how they liked it. She was an expert because one of them slept in close proximity to her, slept two doors down from where she slept in her pink-painted princess bedroom on her pink princess canopy bed.

When I was that age (not that anything is all that different now) I was always kind of anonymous—in every elementary school classroom there was the smart girl, the jock girl, the pretty girl—I was always just "Marnie," nothing more. One day at recess, while Tracey and I were sitting on the pavement eating cups of applesauce, she informed me that she was going to teach me how to kiss boys. I was thrilled to be chosen for the lesson.

Not that I had a boy to kiss, but I figured the earlier I learned the better.

I'm sure there was a certain, specific moment when kissing boys suddenly mattered, but I can't find it in my memory. It could have come along with the same moment my body completely betrayed me via puberty, but I can't remember exactly when that happened either. I feel like I woke up one day and it was all completely different—there were curves and puckered, fleshy fat where familiar angles use to be, and spots and hair growing in where once skin was smooth. And all of a sudden I cared about kissing boys, and liking boys, and making sure that boys liked me too.

It seemed like one day I was running through a sprinkler on our suburban front lawn, flat-chested in a Wonder Woman bathing suit, holding Tracey's pudgy little hand and the next I was mortified by the very idea of being seen. I would hide away in my

THE SMART GIRL

THE JOCK GIRL

THE PRETTY GIRL

room, plucking at my eyebrows and laying out various strategic outfits on the bed to wear to school. I cared so intensely about my appearance that everything else I previously did was disposed of to make room.

If I could have figured out *why* kissing boys mattered so much and remedied that, I wouldn't have a story to tell you at all.

When Tracey kissed me on her pink princess canopy bed when I was eleven years old, I remember she tasted like hotdog mustard and Cheetos. In retrospect, I assume the only reason Tracey had a pink princess canopy bed was because her mother was determined that Tracey would one day be feminine, despite the fact that she was determined to keep her hair cropped short while clad in a pair of ripped overalls.

While Tracey kissed me she moved her head back and forth rapidly and frantically poked her tongue in and out of my mouth.

"You're doing it wrong, Marnie," she said, finally coming up for air.

Tracey wore denim cut-offs with grass stains on the thighs and a pair of blue and red striped socks that always seemed to be soggy and would limply hang from her toes. Her hair was cropped short into a mousy brown bob, and I ran my sparkle-nail-polish-painted fingernails through it while she kissed me, just like she taught me to.

"That's better," she said. "Boys like it when you do it that way."

I likely didn't know it then, but despite the clandestine nature of our practice sessions, it was safe in that bedroom with Tracey.

It was the safest space I had known or would ever come to know. That room was a metaphor—a hybrid of childhood and adolescence, a scene suspended in the precarious space between the two. It was decorated with pink unicorns and stuffed animals, contrasted with pictures of boy bands and assorted cut-outs of waify models from fashion magazines. Tracey even had soft-core porn magazines, a small collection that she'd stolen from her brother's room and hidden under her pink, princess mattress. Together we'd look at the pictures of the plastic, bare-breasted blondes, transfixed by their empty gazes and slightly open mouths. We'd rummage around in her mother's en suite bathroom and she'd paint my face with the resulting booty, mimicking the pouts and come-hither gazes of those semi-clad vixens with poorly applied lip stains and eye pencils. Then, believing ourselves to be beautiful and grown-up, we'd return to our practice in the hopes that one day we could be as exciting as those women pressed snug under the mattress.

Tracey's mother, a hospital nurse with sporadic shifts, eventually came home unannounced and caught us kissing. She heard our girlish giggling and came into the room to ask if we wanted tuna-fish sandwiches. The door to Tracey's bedroom swung open and her mother immediately dropped the two plastic cups full of fruit punch she was carrying. She stared, horrified, as Tracey climbed off me quickly in a futile attempt to act as if nothing had happened. I frantically adjusted my pale yellow sundress, smoothing out the wrinkles while staring at the bright pink pools of punch on the hardwood floor. I couldn't bring myself to look at Tracey's mom. Her rage was evident as she angrily yanked me down the stairs towards the front door.

"Wait until your mother finds out what a dirty, disgusting child you are."

It was then I remembered the make-up, and I rubbed my fist against my lips and cheek to remove it. I could have only looked like a clown—a big pink mouth and my sudden bout of tears bringing about raccoon eyes.

"Get out of here!" Tracey's mother screeched, pointing in the direction of the street.

As I ran down the staircase I could hear Tracey's older brother laughing in the adjacent bedroom while the credits to *Three's Company* rolled on his television. He was older and that meant he got to have a television in his room. He was older and that meant he got to laugh at us whenever he wanted.

My mother was called sometime during the bleak five-minute walk from Tracey's house to mine, a walk I was allowed to do by myself in a time before child kidnapping hysteria and a pervasive fear of sex offenders. During that walk, I recall being terrified that I would suffer a brutal punishment for what Tracey's mother had made me feel was the very, very dirty thing I had done. I didn't entirely understand why our kissing was bad, but I knew something awful was coming.

Yet for whatever reason, that punishment never came.

"Was Tracey teaching you how to kiss boys?" my mother asked me.

I was convinced my mother was the most amazing woman in the world. Her perceived skills included reading my mind.

It was a relief to me that she was smiling. I was seated at our baby blue Formica kitchen table with an extra-large box of Kleenex in front of me, watching her stir a pot of chicken soup n' stars on the stove. Apparently Tracey's mother had stated over the phone that she didn't think it was best that the two of us spend time together for a while. I was devastated and the soup was supposed to remedy this.

"No. She was just trying to get to the other side of the bed and she fell on me," I said through my sobs.

My mother again looked at me knowingly and put her hand on my shoulder. Her long, dark brown hair cascaded around me like a cape as she leaned in to console me.

"It's okay, Marnie. There's nothing wrong with kissing," she said, pouring the soup into my favourite lime green bowl.

She was right, of course, there was and would never be anything wrong with kissing, but that afternoon became a benchmark moment that changed me. That was the moment where all the things that felt safe and good suddenly became dirty and bad, where the soft, tender moments in life became the ones I feared the most.

I never saw the inside of Tracey's pink princess room again, never got to flip through dirty magazines with her, try out new kissing tactics on her or run my fingers through her mousy brown bob. There was no more learning, no more sharing.

After that, things simply, sometimes tragically, *happened* to me.

Tracey and I never spoke again—her mother saw to that by bribing her with promises of horseback riding lessons. One day I cornered her in the girls' bathroom and asked her why she was avoiding me.

"My mother says you're disgusting," was her reply.

After a short period of her averting her gaze whenever I tried to look her in the eye, we grew up and out of elementary school and she ended up going to a different junior high. That took care of any worry her mother had that we'd end up sucking face into our teen years.

I heard from someone that Tracey married a pediatrician when she was only twenty years old and is now a stay-at-home mother of three who is very active in her church group and the PTA.

Meanwhile, I'm almost thirty and I'm still figuring out how to kiss boys.

The urban grocery store is a carnival of loneliness.

Tiny cups of yogurt and tight budget coupon cutting, rolling up and down aisles while averting your eyes from all the other people who don't really see you anyway. They certainly don't want to see you. Single people and single servings, everyone only there out of an animal necessity, a weekly reminder that we are mortal, that we decay as readily as we are created. That we are all so very alone.

I can remember a time when the city was an exciting, crowded, beautifully crazed place for me. I was on the edge of twenty and really felt as if I had escaped something awful in the suburbs. The city meant freedom.

Now it just seems to emphasize how alone we all really are. How free we are to be alone. How alone I am.

I can remember a time before, when I was not this alone. A time before, when I was part of a "we." I got invited to dinner parties and was treated as if I was worth something more simply because I had someone to share my bed with. That's the way the world works; people in partnerships are somehow worth more simply because they have someone to consistently fuck.

When I'm at the grocery store I tend to fidget in the line-up. I eye the contents of my cart with self-loathing.

One apple.
One onion.
One small container of creamer.

Everything I buy is small, self-contained in a serving for one, never risking possible expiry and waste in my studio apartment mini-fridge. Nothing is ever bought in bulk, because there is no one to cook for, no one to share with.

The only creature in my household that gets bulk food is Olive, the tailless rescue cat, her dozens of tins of food too heavy to cart home on foot, her needs necessitating a budget-breaking cab.

Olive's tail was amputated by the shelter vet due to an alleyway infection that occurred prior to adoption. When I make tea in the morning she spins in circles to the tune of the clinking teaspoon, crying at full volume for salmon flavoured cat treats.

Lately her needs seem more important than my own. Her needs are the only ones I ever really care about. Luckily for me her needs are basic.

The upscale, urban grocery store is always overpriced and under-stocked. It is designed poorly, encouraging the chaos of carts and shoppers angrily butting up against each other, trapped in dead end produce aisles and stuck between towers of naturopathic remedies.

It seems it was designed only to make me hate humanity more than I already do.

There are thirty-four items of local produce today. This information is scrawled on a chalk board above a towering pyramid of Red Delicious apples, all of which appear genetically modified to frightening, impossible perfection.

The checkout girl is seventeen and sort-of pretty, knee-deep in her awkward phase, all braces and blemishes and insecurities. While she is bagging my meager purchases I entertain the thought that maybe she envies me and my urban, twenty-something lifestyle, my one apple and my one onion, my bag of cat litter. I am warmed by the fact that maybe she wishes she could be as lonely as I am, craves the kind of aloneness that her meddling parents can't give her, her parents who are tiptoeing through her room while she does her shift at the grocery store. Her mom slowly opening her underwear drawer looking to find a box of condoms or Ziploc bag of weed. Her dad hacking into her Facebook account to find out what boys she's been sending digital kisses to.

But she doesn't envy me, and neither does anyone else in the overpriced and under-stocked carnival. As per usual, I am invisible and generic. I fade and blend into the Campbell's soup can towers and Lipton Sidekick walls.

There are moments where I am tired of being invisible beneath this migraine-inducing fluorescent lighting . There are moments when I want to scream, when I feel like I'll burst and crack open, spraying the gleaming white surfaces with whipped cream and squirting ketchup violently on the tiled floors. There are times when I want to hurl lemons at the bag boy, burst vine-ripened tomatoes under the heel of my boot, spell out "Fuck You" by pouring Olive's kitty litter on the floor of the feminine hygiene aisle.

But I don't.

I am obedient and I avert my gaze as required. While the checkout girl bags my purchases in a brand-new, re-usable, logo emblazoned bag that I am forced to buy because I left mine at home yet again, I stare at the point of purchase items with great intensity. I study myriad colourful packages of chewing gum and assorted tins of lozenges. *US Weekly* lets me know that Britney Spears is partying again, Tori Spelling dropped all that baby weight by eating bread crusts and grapefruit, and that Angelina's mad at Brad over Jen.

Journey's *Don't Stop Believing* plays on the loud speaker above me while the teenage checkout girl takes my Visa card without looking at me, and the phrase "living in a lonely world" strikes me as hilarious, given the circumstance.

I laugh out loud and when I do the checkout girl looks up from affixing a fluorescent orange "paid" sticker to my bag of cat litter, her eyebrow-arched gaze immediately brands me as crazy. I have lost my invisible status and graduated to insane in mere moments, thanks to a tiny outburst of giggles. The other customers behind me take minute steps backward in order to avoid me—to make sure they don't catch whatever urban madness I seem to have contracted from the produce or poultry section. I am immediately shamed and I awkwardly collect my receipt and purchases in order to make a quick escape.

Strangers waiting, up and down the boulevard
Their shadows searching in the night
Streetlight people, living just to find emotion
Hiding, somewhere in the night

I am lonely. I am missing Ben again.

And as I push out the door, I notice that a lone lemon sits invitingly on the top of my reusable shopping bag, begging to be hurled.

THREE

I hide a package of King-size Belmont Milds in a brown wooden box under my queen size bed. I used to hide the fact that I was occasionally smoking them from sanctimonious Ben—after he had finally quit, every time he smelled cigarettes on me he would have this intensely disappointed look on his face that made me feel like a small child.

"But it's because I care about you, Marnie," he would say.

I'll close all the curtains and put out the ashtray on the coffee table. Then I'll open the box very slowly and pull one out, looking over my shoulder to ensure no one is watching, although it's obvious no one is watching me.

Now that Ben's gone I'm not entirely sure who it is I'm hiding my habit from.

Regardless, the shame comes every time I smoke one.

"It's for your own good, Marnie."

The shame comes, but I still enjoy it nonetheless.

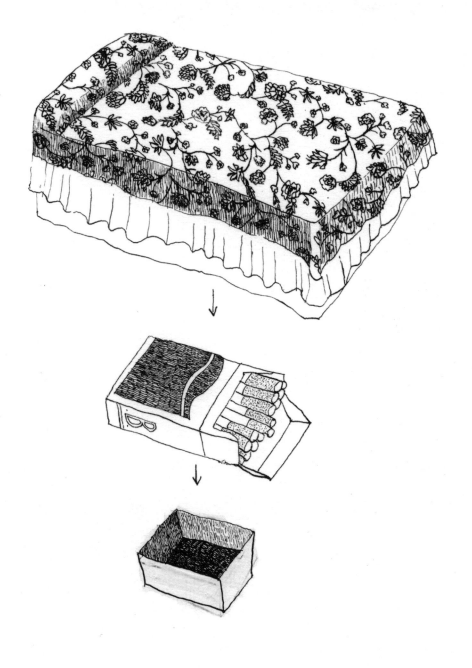

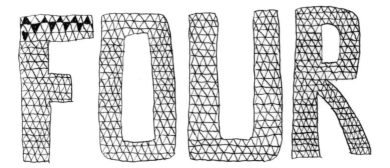

FOUR

I keep a record of how long Ben's been gone on the Ontario Dairy Farmers of Canada sponsored Milk calendar that's attached to my fridge with alphabet magnets. I use a bright red permanent marker to X off the days since he left me.

I feel like I'm counting down the days until I disappear completely. Until the lack of people in my life means I am completely forgotten.

It didn't take long for me to understand that part of growing up is losing companions rather than gaining them. Growing up is about making yourself lonely enough to finally surrender to picking out a single person to spend the rest of your days with. I always hated the fact that growing up meant disposing of room-mates, those strangers and friends you chose as your temporary family, sharing spaces in order to save money.

When I met Ben I was in that space in-between—too old to share space and split rent with friends anymore, but not yet ready to share a bed with someone. Instead, I was alone and admittedly lonely. Perhaps that's why I was vulnerable enough to let him in.

When there isn't a person constantly in your life, a face to wake up to, a voice to remind you who you are or what you should be, you begin to lose a sense of yourself. Even though Ben and I didn't live together, we rarely slept apart. While I certainly don't miss his dirty socks, the way he always left the cap off the tooth-paste, and his tendency to tell me how I should live my life, I do miss him validating the fact that I'm alive.

Life is all routines and rituals when you don't have someone to provide that sacred element of randomness. The surprise of disappointment. Being in love with someone manages to shatter all of your schedules, and when they're gone the void can only be filled with a meticulously designed daily calendar.

When you're alone you become so unseen that your features begin to fade into the wallpaper.

Although people without love don't have wallpaper.

Because you can't have wallpaper without having someone who loves you to help you hang it.

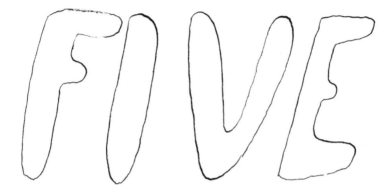

FIVE

At least I have the luxury of my own apartment. Not far from Church and Wellesley, it's small but it's all mine, a tiny room and a half that houses my obsession with compartments—cigar boxes on shelves, clear glass jars that compile trinkets better discarded. I obsessively save all of the evidence that I'm alive, and, when satisfied, collect evidence from the nearby Goodwill that other people are alive as well. I paste every moment of every day into an endless series of ever-fattening scrapbooks. I make endless lists, keeping records of the ebb and flow of a life never actually examined by anyone else.

I file it all away, safe in the knowledge that it proves that, despite the fact no one ever really sees me, I am indeed alive. It all exists to vaguely define me while I feel increasingly invisible.

My name is Marnie and I'm invisible.

Sometimes, when I'm starving for conversation, I'll put on my slippers and go have tea with Neil, the nice old guy across the hall. He is alone and seems to enjoy it, so I'm always hoping some of that will rub off on me. We'll sit in facing armchairs and chat about the weather. Before I leave he'll lend me books, most of which are self-help and spiritual books from the seventies, bought from the discard pile at the Yorkville Branch of the Toronto Public Library.

Actualizing Your True Potential Through Meditation
Learning to Love Yourself More
Cut it Out: Reclaiming Your Me Time in an Age of Distraction
Boundaries: How Saying No Means Saying Yes to Life
Stop! Are the People In Your Life Toxic?

I never read any of them, which should be fairly evident given my inability to actualize anything other than dinner, but I like taking the books anyway. They give me an excuse to go back and return them when I get too lonely, and despite how lame

the books are, with their kitschy seventies cover art and sweep-
ing cursive titles, they give us two practical strangers something
to talk about. I like spending time with Neil; I feel safe and calm
around him, and am never suspect of his motivations for inviting
me over. Since he's a sixty-year-old man living alone near Church
and Wellesley, I just assume he's not interested in anything more
from me than the occasional neighbourly conversation.

"Did you find *Solutions for The Overly Sensitive Person* helpful?"

"Yes, but not as helpful as *A Bold New Approach to Shyness*."

Since Ben left, the majority of the conversations I have daily
are with the cat. Occasionally she'll want something—a cat treat,
the tap turned on so she can drink from it, the glass part of the
window opened so she can climb the screen— and I'll be forced
to figure it out so I can get her to shut up.

Sometimes I stare into my bathroom mirror for great lengths
of time. I study all my distinguishing markings carefully; moles,
spots, scars and the recent appearance of wrinkles; brown eyes,
brown hair, my mother's full cheeks and my father's pale complexion. My mouth is my own.

I am very careful to catalogue all of the things that make me
different from other people. There really aren't that many.

People are constantly telling me, "You know Marnie, you'd be
really pretty if you just—"

What they mean is that I'd be pretty if I was just someone else.

If I am honest with myself I know those things I see in the

mirror are nothing but surface, they make me no different, they are merely incidental.

The things that make me different are the things on the inside. Memories. Like the fact that when I was five, before my little sister Cynthia was born, my dad used to take me out every weekend for walks, just the two of us. That one winter on a walk while my mother was pregnant with my sister I fell through the ice on a frozen pond in a park near our house—that it cracked open around me and I plunged right in. Although that pond was likely only waist deep, my father crawled across the ice on his stomach to pull me out.

A heavy, wet, sinking weight, his only daughter entrapped in a soggy pink snowsuit, screaming.

I'm different because as distant as my father is now, I've never forgotten that he pulled me from that pond, and that he then ran quickly and calmly across a snow-covered field towards our house with me in his arms.

I remember that later that evening when I was supposed to be sleeping I sat at the top of the stairs in my favourite Scooby-Doo pyjamas, listening to him cry, and I watched my mother console him in a rare moment of vulnerability from a man who never flinched, never cared, never complimented me.

If I hadn't fallen through that pond when I was five years old I would have lived with the insecurity that he loved my baby sister Cynthia more. Cynthia, six years younger than me, was the golden child—a smart and pretty petite blonde who always came home on holidays from Queen's University with fantastic news.

"I have fantastic news," she would shriek wildly as she came in the front door with her suitcase.

A boyfriend in law school. A high paying prestigious summer job. A 3.9 GPA.

Both my sister and my father always contributed to that feeling of fading into the wallpaper.

It was okay that he never told me he loved me. That memory of being pulled from a waist-deep pond was enough to carry me through life with the knowledge that he did. If it wasn't for that memory, I would always feel entirely mediocre.

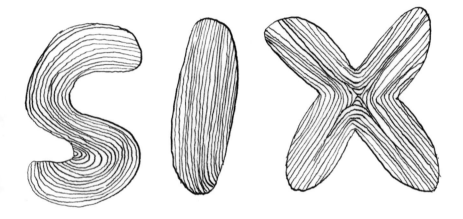

Sometimes I secretly wish I was suicidal, if only so I wouldn't be so constantly afraid of death.

Sometimes I wish for nothing more than the feeling of satisfaction.

Sometimes I wish for someone thoroughly toxic to come into my life, someone who can remind me why I chose to be alone in the first place.

SEVEN

The story of how Ben and I met is a story I can no longer tell over cocktails to curious strangers.

At one point it was a story I loved to tell, a story I told often, but when you are alone people get uncomfortable with impromptu, nostalgic tales of now long gone exes. Talking about the night Ben and I met, about the full moon and the perfect snowfall, simply doesn't qualify as "moving on."

But if I was allowed, this is how I would tell the story of how Ben and I met:

Ben and I met because of someone else's break up. Not the best way to procure a partner, but in some ways, it's the only way we ever really procure a partner. Logically, we only ever have someone because someone else doesn't, so meeting over a break up, even someone else's, is as good a reason as any to fall in love.

Don't we only ever really have someone until someone else does, anyway? With Ben, it always seemed like someone else, someone more interesting and less exhausting, was meant to have him. And now they do.

Sharon, a girlfriend of mine, had broken up with Tyler for the sixth time that year. This particular break up was prompted by a pile of laundry that wasn't done, and an argument that escalated into a screaming match about what she called his "Mommy complex."

Sharon's heart was broken again and she loved the attention that afforded her, so she had invited her twenty-person support system down to her local bar on Front Street to buy her martinis while she sniffled dramatically into her sleeve. As a group we were generally of the collective mindset that break ups—not marriages, babies or even deaths—warranted the greatest amount of money spent on friends, so I left my east end apartment and withdrew one hundred dollars from an ATM, preparing myself with speeches about fish in the sea.

On the west side of town, Ben did the same.

It was January. It was snowing. It wasn't that cold.

I had somehow never met Ben while we were sharing Sharon as a friend. He was a charmingly dishevelled, green-eyed boy who played bass in a band called "Clifford," a boy who liked both Kirkegaard and the Transformers, wore a lot of corduroy, smoked Gauloises and ate macrobiotic foods. He dug graves at a cemetery for a living and wrote song lyrics for pleasure. He lived in a three-bedroom apartment on the first floor of a house in Parkdale with two of his band mates and a 120-pound grey mottled mastiff named Bill, who was rescued in a police drug raid on a heroin operation.

(I later learned that I preferred Bill to the band mates, primarily because the dog smelled better and was less likely to accidentally disturb us while we were having sex.)

Ben was beautiful in his own vaguely unhygienic and occasionally irresponsible way. He smelled like stale cigarettes and wet wood, and his threadbare clothes seemed like they didn't fit quite right, but he was perfect and for some reason, he immediately thought the same of me.

"You're adorable," he said while offering me a whiskey shot.

Puppy adorable or let's rip each other's clothes off adorable?

After a good number of drinks and Gauloises were consumed between us, I considered the quality of my current underwear (black lace—a rare occurrence) and decided to take Ben home with me. While the snow fell in massive flakes around us and found a home in our hair and on our shoulders, Ben lovingly and

35

delicately touched my frozen cheek and nodded enthusiastically. He then proceeded to throw up all over the sidewalk outside the bar.

I stroked his back as he hunched over gagging, secretly enjoying this new feeling of taking care of someone else, someone else who might return the favour later. When he was done he looked up at me, wiped his mouth with his corduroy sleeve, and asked me if the invitation was still open.

By morning Ben was my new boyfriend.

Sharon got back together with Tyler thirty-six hours later.

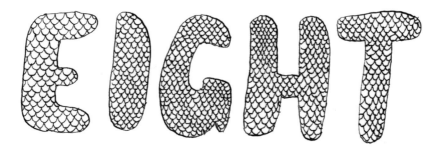

EIGHT

On the streetcar at noon there is a woman yelling at herself.

I watch her scream as the other passengers avert their eyes. I would yell at myself along with her if I had her courage. We could yell at ourselves together.

But I am, or at least Ben has told me that I am, *passive aggressive*.

Because I am *passive aggressive*, instead of screaming at myself I quietly carved his name into the paper white of my left inner thigh with a sterling silver letter opener I stole from the office supply closet at work. Three days ago I carved the three letters into my thigh while hiding in a salmon pink workplace bathroom stall. The stain and strain of this pink marking is now yelling much like this courageous woman, the *passive aggressive* itch of three letters screaming at the inside of my blue jeans at noon on a city streetcar at the corner of Sherbourne and Queen.

For a living I file things, file them so I can be paid, file them so I can eat.

I file papers and numbers, documents and charts, pieces of a pointless history put in multicoloured folders and stored away snugly in heavy metal filing drawers.

Occasionally I wonder why I do this, why I waste the hours to get money to eat if no one ever opens these heaving, lonely drawers but me, the papers and numbers forever lost inside. The megalomaniac narcissist who is my boss insists that I capture every minute, every moment of our organization, colour code each event of each day and carefully label each meaningless movement for a posterity never to be viewed.

While I file all these mundane details, I simultaneously cata- logue my multicoloured memories, coding and labelling them, knowing that they will be locked tight in the heavy metal draw- ers of my mind and viewed only by me in moments of liquored misery and ecstasy. Never to be screamed out on city streetcars at the corner of Sherbourne and Queen.

I stole that letter opener from the office supply closet because I loathe this fucking filing and the fucking feeling of being on my knees in a storage room for the good of a pointless posterity. I stole the letter opener because Ben left me and I was angry and I thought if I could make that anger visible it would go away.

I want the inside of my thigh to remember so that I can forget. I want to close the filing drawer and hear its click, hear that its multicoloured and carefully coded secrets are safe inside. No stains or strains yelling from the past, just the three letters of his name quietly and passively carved, now healing, aggressively whispering into the paper white of my thigh and the blue of my jeans.

NINE

Lately I've been collecting and accumulating fears of dying.

Being alone means I've got a lot more time on my hands to pay attention to all the ways I could possibly go. Being alone means I've got a lot more time to fantasize about all the ways no one will likely notice.

I make a point to write down my pervasive panic daily, carrying with me a little brown dog-eared notebook and cataloguing the things that rattle me, a rapidly growing list of all my obsessive anxieties. For some reason, having them documented makes me feel more in control of the possibility they will arise. Having a record means at some point I can say, "see, I told you so."

While "cancer" shows up on these lists almost daily, other items rotate, appear and disappear at will, things like "bladder infection" and "sudden paralysis."

Then there are the more irrational fears, like "attacked by pigeons" and "pushed onto subway tracks."

I jot them all down on the same pages I write lists of "things to do," how many cigarettes I've smoked, and phone numbers I need to recall. What results is randomized combinations of digits, dentist appointments and descriptions of tsunamis and tornados, reminders of Friday night dates and an overwhelming fear of scabies.

Like little pseudo-haikus of the modern neurotic condition:

Thursday, Meeting about new digital filing system, 10:30 a.m.
Eye Abscess, Colon Cancer, Eaten by Wild Dogs
Pick up eggs, milk and cat food
8

Olive; Veterinary Appointment, Monday 9:45 a.m.
Fainting on the bus, blood clot in leg, pregnancy, female pattern baldness
Call Ben at work: 416 767 8923
3

Fear of Fighting

Return Ben's Sweater and DVDs
Being alone
Buy Vodka
17

Today I am concerned I have colon cancer.
Yesterday it was psoriasis.
The day before that everyone hated me and was talking about me behind my back. Tomorrow there will be abscesses and lawsuits, gossiping and growths.
The day after that I will have a seizure in line at the post office. While I'm having that seizure, I will be fired via voicemail and my bike will be stolen.
My body betrays me. My moles are "changing." My breasts are simply dormant containers, waiting for the delivery of disease. Occasionally, I contemplate removing everything that waits to become broken. In my mind my insides are simply anticipating damage and destruction. My jaw doesn't fit together right. The strange feeling in my mouth means mouth cancer. Every ache and pain is a harbinger of disease. Walk-in clinic doctors despise me and turn me away; they tell me I am taking up their time with my inability to swallow and my "feelings of fuzziness."
I do have those rare days when I feel healthy and clean inside and very much alive. But all it takes is one person to pass me in the street, a person with a visible sign of disease painted on their face, a swollen eye or crooked scar, a malformed growth or

broken front tooth, and I am back in that place. I meet someone who broke their collarbone by falling off a curb or someone who caught a bad case of warts from a tanning bed and I'm petrified again. That feeling of dread overwhelms me and I am gone. My mind is consumed with what is possible, and never with what is probable.

It's all chronic ailments and secret fears realized. Every moment, every meeting, every conversation, tainted by the fact that I am certain I will perish in a sudden tragedy.

I am amazed by the few tiny moments I am not afraid.

In fact, I am amazed at every day I am still alive.

I think I got the office job in the first place because I became comfortable with having no identity. I also think the temp agency could sense that about me when they met me and that's why they sent me there. I arrived at their sparse office with their generic, grey furniture and a grey man in a cheap grey suit said, "Marnie, you'd be perfect in accounts receivable" and handed me a sheet of paper with an address on it.

To be honest I was thankful—the logical next step in erasing myself completely was a job as mind numbing and pointless as the one he had just given me. Accounts receivable is the perfect corporate depository for someone who is essentially invisible.

The fact that I'm a wallpaper kind of girl is not a new phenomenon. I've always been an extra in the movie that is someone else's fantastic life. People "accidentally" step in front of me in line-ups, genuinely saying, "oh sorry, I didn't see you there." If you met me at a party I wouldn't be all that memorable and you'd certainly have a hard time describing me in retrospect. I'd be "that girl," although it's unlikely you'd have a reason to need to remember me anyway

I'm an afterthought embodied. I'm not tall and I'm not short. I'm not fat and I'm not thin. My one real distinguishing feature—a face full of freckles—I manage to blot out with a compact of pressed powder I carry with me constantly. I wear neutral, earth-toned items of clothing—jeans and t-shirts, button down shirts and flat shoes. I have mid-length brown hair—not chestnut or clove, hazelnut or cinnamon stick, but *brown*. Although I've attempted to dye it numerous times, I've never used a permanent colour, only the kind that washes out in twenty-eight shampoos.

As a result, I am constantly washed out, consistently fading, flat and colourless. Not one vibrant characteristic to distinguish my identity from the rest.

Perfect for a job in the accounts receivable department.

Maybe my lack of identity was a reason I got (and lost) Ben as well, but I feel the need to explain the office job and have never felt the need to explain Ben. Ben was beautiful and as a choice, self-explanatory. He filled in the parts of me that were missing —which in the end turned out to be a whole lot of parts. Ben, with his band and his big grey dog and badass yet virtuous behavior, made me more interesting. On the surface the office job did nothing for me. It was mediocre, bland and in constant need of excusing.

Excuses included the usual "health benefits" or "it's only temporary" or "I'm between things."

Thanks to the generic grey-suited man at the temp agency, I got an interview in the accounts receivable department of Wood-chuck Shredding Services—"specializing in hard copy data obliteration." Woodchuck owned a fleet of trucks that drove around the city to pick up and deliver confidential files for secure disposal. Credit card numbers and blood test results, personal histories and personal mistakes—all the things that people wanted to hide, destroy or pretend never happened. I never saw any of the files, of course, but I was fascinated by the notion that people paid me to ensure their secrets were safely obliterated. Every time I spoke to a client about their account I fantasized endlessly about what they were hiding. I imagined their secret, paralyzing fears of Revenue Canada, ex-wives, hackers and identity thieves.

When I went for the obligatory "it's just a formality" interview at the offices of Woodchuck Shredding Services I deliberately went without any hint of a personality. I wore a brown dress, drugstore pantyhose and very little make-up. I decided I would simply be whatever they wanted me to be and it turned out they wanted me to be no one. They wanted me to be invisible. Something I was very good at.

They hired me in the first fifteen minutes of the interview and I didn't disappoint. I went on to perfect invisibility.

The sole purpose of Woodchuck Shredding Services was to shred paper, and my job was to make sure people paid their shredding bills. I existed as part of a flawless machine and rarely interacted with any of the other parts. There were never any staff lunches or beers after work for me. My desk was in the bowels of a towering glass high-rise in the financial district, and under the flicker of migraine-inducing fluorescent lights, I wore my signature drugstore pantyhose and the bland, brown knee-length skirts that were required of me. I filed the paperwork and made the phone calls to outstanding account holders. I did all of this completely alone, day in and day out, only occasionally interacting with my detestable bitch of a boss who I made every effort to avoid.

I never really knew who I was or who I planned to be, so being stuck in the perpetual solitude and flickering greyness that was a nondescript desk job seemed fitting enough. I made no effort to decorate the desk with anything that might expose who I was to anyone who might care. No pictures of Ben or Olive, no cutouts of amusing comic strips or printouts of inspirational quotes. Keep-

ing my sense of self out of my cubicle meant that the accounts receivable department never had to define who I was inside, and I liked the mindlessness, the impersonality of it all. I was both indispensable and invisible. I liked having the quiet to fantasize about a better life. I liked leaving it all there at the end of the day. I liked stealing things from the office supply closet.

Watching the account executives fish the recesses of their minds for my name when they gave me filing or phoning directions amused me. I smiled knowingly when some of them couldn't come up with it and instead faked their way through conversations with me. Others simply didn't try at all and instead called me Maggie or Mary. I never cared enough to correct them—I simply filed their financial records and collected my pay cheque. I was fully aware of the pointless nature of what I did for a living and I tolerated that simply because I couldn't bring myself to define myself otherwise.

"Good job on those income reports, Molly."

The job was perfect until I couldn't bring myself to get up and go to it anymore. When that particular brand of Ben-induced neurosis set in, I simply left a message on an answering machine stating my intention to never set foot in Woodchuck Shredding Services again.

And no one ever called me back.

ELEVEN

The first and only time I ever really fell in love I was a twenty-one
-year-old art school student. I was studying painting and drawing for no other reason than it seemed to make me interesting.
It did make me interesting, and someone fell in love with me as
a result.

I was young and I was foolish and it was perfect. I know, now,
that every day was perfect then—it was a time where everything

was both monumentally tragic and triumphant, a time when every thing was simultaneously possible and impossible, a time before life became a series of investment strategies and chiropractic appointments.

University life was constantly filmic and devastating, and because it was art school, always seemed to involve alcohol.

The first time I ever fell in love I was twenty-one and I put a cigarette out on my arm when he finally told me he loved me back. We were standing in a crowded bar on McCaul Street and the drinks were plentiful and potent, and I suddenly decided to create a very physical marker to remember that moment of first love. He likely didn't really love me and maybe I didn't even really love him either, but it didn't matter and it still doesn't. I was *in* love and it was perfect.

I remember the skin on the inside of my wrist singed so quickly, blistered pink and then red as the burn took shape in the smoke that surrounded it. I looked straight into his eyes as I did it and felt nothing but a love so vast I must have been falling face first into it.

The boy's eyes were blue and he had an English accent with which he always called me "My Marianne." Together we drank shots of Goldschläger to celebrate and eventually he took me home with him. When we got there he sat me down on the edge of his bathtub in order to perform first aid on the cigarette burn and I watched adoringly as he applied aloe vera gel and wrapped my wrist gently in gauze. He was beautiful and I never wanted the

moment to end, wanted him to heal every tiny wound I had for the rest of my days.

Then we went to his bedroom and he put on some bad techno so we could fuck without his roommates hearing us.

I naïvely thought he was the person I was meant to live out the rest of my days with, but eventually we destroyed each other the way people who say *I love you* often do. In the spring, when everything was alive and growing again, he killed any notion of *us* dead by meeting someone else. He broke up with me in an airport, at the arrival gate on the day I came back from a week-long spring break trip to Paris.

I didn't see it coming nor was I prepared for the misery that ensued. It was love and then it was over, and I was determined to make sure it never happened again. That marking on my right wrist would always act as a reminder of that.

Seven years later I still have that scar. Seven years later I feel so old.

I stare at the perfect circle on my right wrist and wonder if anything will ever again permeate my level of apathy the way that blue-eyed boy with a British accent did at a bar when I was twenty-one.

With that scar on my wrist, the lesson I learned was that hopeless romanticism (just like painting and drawing and art school) doesn't pay the bills, nor does it satiate the need to be fed and clothed. Growing up consisted of this stream of lessons, the kind that erased the magic punctuated by Goldschläger shots, drowned it out with the grating repetition of bill collectors and late student loan payments. I no longer had youthful illusions and I knew that any temporary escape was simply that, and it was with this knowledge that I consciously avoided the car crashes of love and sex. But as I crept into my mid and then into my late twenties, I yearned to again have the kind of love that was like poetry slipped through the gaps in high-school locker doors.

When everything was simultaneously possible and impossible.

A perfect circle, burned into the inside of my right wrist.

TWELVE

Even after I met Ben I still wanted to be alone. Being alone was safe and predictable. Even with that initial bliss of kissing him in those fat flakes of snow, I knew all too well that it was dangerous. With love came a fleeting promise of happiness that would later mean nothing but unhappiness.

One night, after I had reluctantly started dating Ben, I decided to walk home alone from a bar in the Annex. I was out with a group of friends who all lived in another part of town, and it was after last call and the subway had closed, so I decided to head east on Bloor towards the Village. I'd had just enough drinks to ensure that I thought that this was a very good idea but not enough drinks to make the trip too difficult to endure. It was cold, and my feet were aching in my higher than usual heels, but the walk and the air and the night felt empowering. I was free from the need to be attached to anyone, as if I never needed anyone to take care of me, certainly not Ben. With my headphones in and my heels on, I was invincible.

And in that very moment of invincibility, a man ran past me, and as he did, grabbed my oversized brown leather purse and attempted to pull it from my shoulder.

And I didn't let go.

I didn't let go because the moment was mine and he wasn't going to steal it along with my purse. My reluctance to surrender my bag is certainly not recommended, but that walk home was the first time I felt completely free: I was drunk but I was also liberated from the notion that I needed someone else to tell me everything was going to be okay. So there was no way I was letting go of that feeling along with my purse, no way I was going to suffer that loss only to prove that I needed the help of someone other than myself.

Then I felt my wrist snap in the moment I hit the pavement.

The pain was searing and immediate, but I was still incapable of releasing my grip on the bag. As I lay on the sidewalk the man (who I had not even had a moment to attempt to look at) decided to pull me five feet through the salt, slush and gravel in his determination to retrieve my handbag, causing me to lose my left shoe. Events suddenly ran in slow motion, affording me the time to consider the apparently precious contents of my handbag:

A circular tin of pocket size Vaseline Petroleum Jelly Lip Therapy
A $32 receipt from Dollarama
Bach's Rescue Remedy
Two Condoms, both expired
A used copy of William Somerset Maugham's Of Human Bondage
Herbacin hand cream
Three fruit candies, complimentary with the bill of last night's
Vietnamese dinner with Ben (date #3)
One o.b. tampon,
A notebook
A paperclip
A hair elastic,
A black ballpoint pen
A scratch and win card
A wallet containing $6.47 in cash, a Visa card, an expired driver's
license, and a ticket stub to a 1998 Depeche Mode concert.

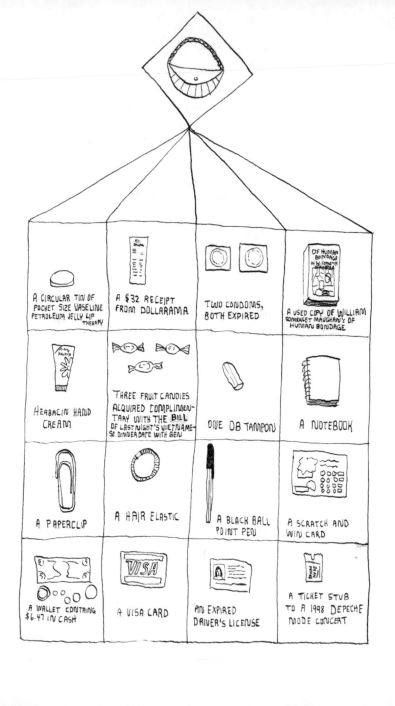

Eventually he surrendered, perhaps realizing that pulling me five feet along the pavement was not going to get him any closer to his goal of acquiring my $6.47 in cash. Yet the brief moment of joy I felt, from the success associated with his rapid retreat, was soon overwhelmed by the intense pain in my now fractured wrist. I was drunk enough to assume I could handle the pain of a broken wrist on my own, but sober enough to abandon the once brilliant idea of walking home by myself. I looked down at the sludge that completely covered the front of my winter parka and noticed a hole that had been torn in my nylons. I hopped on one foot back to my shoe.

I used my left arm to hail a cab, and asked the driver to get me to an ATM so I could retrieve the other $8.53 necessary to get home.

"Are you okay?" he asked. The pain was apparent on my face and I was, of course, covered in dirt.

"Never better," I winced.

When I got home to my apartment (and after some difficulty unlocking and opening the front door with one hand), I for some reason assumed there would be a bag of peas or carrots in the freezer, despite the fact that I had never purchased a frozen vegetable of any kind the entire time I had lived there. When I opened the freezer the only thing on offer was a half empty forty ounce bottle of Absolut vodka. I tucked it under my right armpit and unscrewed the cap with my good hand, taking a swig before applying the cool bottle to my now swelling right wrist.

I lay on the living room floor, too tired to undress or even remove my shoes, pressing the frozen bottle to my swollen wrist before I finally fell asleep. Before I drifted off into a drunken slumber I finally felt capable. I was invincible, not invisible.

A feeling that, thanks to Ben's sudden appearance in (and later disappearance from) my life, would never return.

The next morning I put the vodka back in my empty freezer and called Ben to ask him if he would come with me to the emergency room.

THIRTEEN

I didn't want anybody but instead I got Ben. And I slept with Ben immediately and loved Ben instantly. My capacity to love instantly and fall quickly was the reason I didn't want anybody in the first place.

But instead I got Ben.

It was evident Ben liked women. He had a vast collection of shredded love letters and photographs and kept the resulting confetti in the wooden cigar boxes that lined his windowsill. He had also amassed a small collection of discarded girl's garments, silk stockings and pink angora cardigans and pale blue camisoles, crammed in dresser drawers next to his frayed and flawed wool and corduroy. He had quite a collection of telling collectables, a cache of conquests to keep him warm during winter hibernation.

He lined his shelves with books I'd never read and couldn't read. Books I wouldn't read even if I could have.

That snowfall played tricks on me.

It forced him inside me, frayed collar and cuffs, suspicious collections and all.

FOURTEEN

Where did he end and where did I begin? It was always impossible
to tell, on a Friday afternoon when we'd both called in sick so we
could have sex and watch cartoons. A Friday afternoon when the
bed was a borderland and a toe to the floor was treason. There
were entire days spent naked, food delivered, love made. We did
mushrooms and listened to Motown, barbecued hotdogs on his
back porch while Bill watched, salivating.

With Ben, skin was frontier and words no longer translated, we simply hummed to a rhythm in the perfect afternoon light. I lost all my boundaries with him; there was no feeling of end, no lines drawn in chalk to outline *us and them, you and me*. Everything became everything else, blended and bleeding like a watercolour stain, gradations of light and dark.

Afternoons in bed with Ben would be a blur of sleeping and waking. Ben would step into the shower and I would wake momentarily in his absence. With my palm I would lovingly smooth flat the half of the fitted sheet that was still warm with his body. Through the wall I could hear pipes rumble with water pressure. I would watch Bill sleep in a patch of sunlight on the floor of the bedroom, spluttering out his dreams of fighting, chasing and running from his enormous jaw, his paws twitching in an epic imagined race.

When we would finally decide to get up it was usually when afternoon had become evening, and we'd take the dog on a long walk to Trinity Bellwoods and throw a ball for him. While the sun went down, we'd share a cigarette and an extra large slurpee from the 7-11 while Bill wrestled a twenty-pound boston terrier who fancied himself tough enough to take him on.

My overpowering love for Ben made me do things like make mixtapes and write love notes. On our first Valentine's Day I surprised him by putting sparkly heart-shaped red stickers on every item in his fridge. For weeks we made Sunday morning omelettes with love-branded eggs.

I always knew one day it would end, that I could only pretend to be interesting and pretty enough for so long. After I accepted that, I was able to relax and enjoy ice cream and war movies while he had his arm around me.

If Ben did anything, he helped me to live in the present tense. When I was with him, tossing tennis balls and sipping slurpees was all I ever needed.

FIFTEEN

Bill, the mastiff, made a habit of curling into the space between Ben and I while we slept, which was quite an achievement for a dog of his size. Having the beast snuggled into the crooks of our elbows and knees was an endearing practice that I never argued against unless it somehow interfered with sex. I had a strict rule that Bill was never, ever allowed to see us having sex—half because it disturbed me and half because I thought it might permanently disturb the dog.

"But Bill has seen lots of—" Ben had started to argue one night while things were getting heated and we were at the point of my bra being removed. I stopped him immediately with a finger to his mouth. Bill was then dragged by his red leather spiked collar out the bedroom door.

One night I woke up next to Bill in Ben's bed with searing, stomach-splitting pains. I opened my eyes to see his large tongue lolling out of his mouth, his eyes rolled back in his head while he snored loudly. Without much thought I leapt out of bed and proceeded to beeline for the bathroom with the dog's big, lumbering body trudging along behind me.

After I had managed to expel the entirety of the Chinese food takeout Ben had ordered earlier that evening, he appeared at the bathroom door. After getting on his knees next to me and putting his hand on my back, he suggested that we just go straight to the hospital.

"No, no really, I'm totally—"

The pains returned and I was back to emptying my stomach. With my forehead resting on the edge of the toilet bowl I managed to meekly nod in agreement with the hospital plan while Bill enthusiastically licked my chin.

"Think of it this way," Ben said. "If we don't go to the hospital, you're going to get a bruise on your forehead."

Because of that night, my definition of love grew to include feeling comfortable enough to vomit in front of someone.

Ben was always like that—logical and cool, and mostly hilarious under any kind of pressure. While I would spend hours sweating and moaning dramatically on the bathroom tiles, he would recommend we go get a professional to deal with the matter. He was by my side when the food poisoning stole my dignity from me in the ER waiting room, holding both my hand and my plastic bucket.

A little blonde girl in a lavender dress, about four years old, sat across from me in the waiting room, clutching a stuffed giraffe and her mother's arm. While the mother seemed terrified that there was something wrong with her daughter, the little girl, instead, seemed terrified by the sound of my constant retching. She hid her face behind her mother's arm so she wouldn't have to witness me hunched over in a brown plastic waiting room chair, gripping my stomach in humiliating, defeating agony. Ben attempted to smile at the girl to reassure her and said, perhaps to both of us, "It'll be over soon."

I always relied on Ben to tell me when the pain would be over.

When it's all over, when it's all broken, what happens then? We're suddenly expected to start all over again, with everything all smashed and ruined. We're expected to drag our pathetic selves to the next available body and say, "Here, this is all fucked up, but you can have it."

Here, I dare you to try to unbreak what is broken.

When I came out from seeing the doctor, Ben was sitting on the floor of the waiting room with the little girl, reading her a story about monkeys in the jungle while her mother discussed something with the nurse at the desk.

He introduced me to Suzy, his new four-year-old friend.

"You ate something bad," she said, looking up at me with her enormous blue eyes.

"Yes, but I'm feeling better now," I replied, smiling meekly.

"You wanna know a secret?" Suzy suddenly whispered, jumping to her feet and reaching to pull me towards her.

"He loves you. He told me so," she said.

Now, without someone to love me, I often think that I couldn't suffer the indignity of food poisoning alone.

I often buy books that I feel would help Marnie, but mostly I just buy them so I have a reason to invite her over. I realize that she's a good thirty years younger than me, but I've become pretty good at pretending that doesn't matter. I love having her sit across from me in my apartment, love her awkward beauty and the way she nervously twirls her hair between her fingertips. If that's all I'm ever going to get, so be it.

One week when I invited Marnie over she told me she wasn't well, that she had gone to the hospital for a "procedure." But the walls are thin and I knew exactly what was wrong.

The next day I bought her a book about dealing with loss and left it on her welcome mat.

SEVENTEEN

The second month Ben and I were together I got pregnant. I was pregnant and we had only just graduated to sleepovers and hand-holding in public.

The bliss I felt in meeting (and fucking) him was destroyed as soon as I peed on that store-bought test. Suddenly I detested him and his lack of hygiene, his Kirkegaard and his bass guitar. I sat cross-legged on the floor in the middle of my one-room apartment and Olive meowed and rubbed her head anxiously against my left knee while I stared at the test with complete disbelief. I was hoping that if I stared at it longer the likelihood that it was completely wrong, or a joke, would increase. That the plus sign would become a minus sign, and Ben and I could gracefully go back to "taking things slowly." Back to spending long, naked days in bed with take-out and *Back to the Future* on DVD.

But that pink plus sign meant nothing would ever again go slowly.

It's difficult to tell someone that you really just met that you're carrying their potential offspring, and I considered not telling Ben at all. It would have been easy enough to deal with things and never have him be aware of what I had done. Besides, his entire persona was dependant on the fact that he was a grown-up child who read smart-people books but still liked cartoons and foosball. He wasn't a father and wasn't going to be a father. Informing him of his part in some frantic cell division that happened to be going on inside me seemed futile. Literally fruitless.

From my perspective on the floor with that store-bought test there was something living off me for nothing more than nutrients, it was parasitic, inducing feelings of panic and nausea, and I wanted it gone. And I tried to be as unemotional about it being gone as possible.

At least, that was the perspective that made it easier to cope. I attempted to ignore a nagging feeling in my gut that wanted it to be possible, but as much as I didn't want to name it, or shop for it, or fantasize about its landmark life events, it was impossible not to consider Ben as "Daddy."

To cope I used horrifying, shame-filled phrases like "get it taken care of."

When I told Ben, who was generally animated and expressive, he developed an uncharacteristically blank look. I couldn't have figured out his feelings on the subject if I tried—not that I had the vaguest interest in trying.

When it came to my uterus and its recent inhabitant, he was irrelevant, and I told him so.

I booked an appointment and Ben asked the cemetery for the day off. He came with me like the dutiful partner he turned out to be, and he was intuitive about my need for silence. Before the procedure we were both required to endure a stock discussion about our "options"

You need to ask yourself some questions, Marnie. You need to ask yourself:

What is going on in my life?
What are my plans for the future?
What are my spiritual and moral beliefs?
What do I believe is best for me in the long run?
Which choice(s) could I live with?
Which choice(s) would be impossible for me?
How would each choice affect my everyday life?
What would each choice mean to the people closest to me?

There weren't choices. I wanted it out of me. I wanted it over.

Ben just nodded and endured and shared no feelings on the matter. While the plump, pleasant woman at the clinic spoke calmly and kindly he simply fidgeted with frayed cuffs and tapped his foot nervously.

"Whatever you want, Marnie," he said repeatedly. Robotically.

When we told the counsellor at the clinic how long we had been together she said that she would have guessed it was much longer. I immediately, inappropriately, laughed out loud after she said so.

After it was over I felt relief. The rest was numbness. Ben took me home, tucked me in his bed and made me tomato soup. He went to the store to get me some maxi pads and a litre of Ben and Jerry's. While he was gone, Bill put his enormous head on my stomach and looked at me with his enormous, sad eyes, devastated.

That was the first and only time that I cried, a moment that was witnessed only by the dog and that ended before Ben's return from the store.

Two days after I had the abortion, a Wednesday, Ben drank eleven beers in one night, four of which he consumed at a bar by himself after his companions had decided to go home. On his way to the subway after last call he put his fist through the front window of a McDonalds and sliced open his wrist. The hospital called me at three in the morning because he told them I was his "wife" and I watched stoically as he got three stitches and a scolding by an overly earnest young female doctor.

"We're having a baby," he told her while she clipped the final stitch.

I hated him.

"Congratulations," she said, abruptly snapping off her latex glove. She looked at me knowingly and rolled her eyes.

The next week, Ben announced that he was quitting smoking.

EIGHTEEN

"God, can you fucking clone him?"

My friend Adrian takes me out for a long lunch, and by Thursday it is my third long lunch of the week. Not that Woodchuck ever notices I am gone.

Adrian and I dated in high school. He was the first to fumble with my bra strap and bravely unbutton the top button of my over-dyed red jeans, circa 1994. Ten years later, Adrian is gay and I am apparently dating the man of his dreams.

This reaction to Ben was a common one among my friends, making it difficult for me to explain why Ben made me so uncomfortable with his perfection. With how impenetrable his perfection appears.

On the bus on the way to lunch there was a baby swaddled in a snowsuit, its limbs absurdly jutting out, mummified in its protective purple shell, a casing sealed tightly with a matching purple scarf. The baby gurgled and kicked wildly, its giggles piercing the damp dog scented air in an otherwise quiet bus.

Sometimes I think about babies, and then about Ben, and then about the fact that a boy with a band who lives in a three-bedroom apartment in Parkdale with friends is not ready for a baby.

And then I think about the fact that I'm almost thirty.

I like to fantasize about a life as an independent modern girl, living alone with a grey and white temperamental cat, scrawling myriad appointments in a sporadically highlighted date book, but babies on buses kick at the gears and springs of the biological clock in my gut. While I watch them gurgle and shriek I wonder if carefully snowsuit-swaddled babies know in their soft skulls what I'm thinking, and if they perform just for me and my insecurities. Tiny Velcro shoes tapping out the tune of my want.

Babies, with their delicious faces and excruciatingly long lashes; do they know how they are coveted by those who have falsely embraced a life of singularity?

I can't even take care of my cat.

"Marnie, are you even listening to me?"

Adrian never thinks about babies. He thinks about raunchy online m4m personal ads and even raunchier one night stands. He thinks about whether or not my shoes match my sweater, or if my new lipstick shade makes me look pale. Whether or not leopard print or black nail polish is "so last year."

"You don't look well, Marnie. Do you want an Atavan?"

Adrian is constantly shoving a fistful of pharmaceuticals at me, believing that *the modern condition* can only be cured with a prescription.

I look at my watch. Technically I am late for filing.

"Adrian, I should really get back to work," I say anxiously.

"Oh, shut up and stay for another, Marnie."

And I do. And another. And when the bill arrives, I no longer wonder about babies but instead wonder if I have enough money in my wallet to pay it. I toss an Atavan into my mouth and gulp back some white wine.

"Thatta girl," Adrian says.

NINETEEN

I tried to be Ben's "cool girlfriend." This meant that I tried to be understanding and not say *I love you* too much and never act like I cared when he was late. I tried not to obsess about every word and every action, every phone call and every kiss.

But if I was honest, there was nothing remotely cool about me.
If I was honest, this is what I would have said:

I get drunk and browse eBay for wedding dresses even though
I am publicly against marriage and have been known to call it "an
oppressive cultural fallacy of female entrapment." I have written
my first name attached to your last name in cursive handwriting
in my notebook. I even drew a heart around it.

I download and masturbate to lesbian porn constructed for
and marketed to straight men, but make sure the cat is secure
in the next room. After I am done I feel like I have betrayed you.
And Olive.

I am annoyed that you have never once had a shower at my
place.

I am still smoking despite the fact that I told you I quit twenty-
nine days ago.

Although I am outwardly cool about all of your friends being
very attractive, very stylish, primarily single women (groupies)
who think you are wonderful, I am not. Cool about it. At all.

I do not actually think it is "cute when you're grumpy." I said
this because it gives the appearance of me being understanding
when you're being an asshole.

When I blurted out the words *I love you* that one time when we
were having "crazy monkey sex" I actually called all of my friends
and had a whiskey fuelled summit meeting regarding what I
should do about it. It was only when Adrian informed me that
saying *I love you* during sex makes a man feel like he (and I quote)

I AM TRYING TO BE
YOUR COOL GIRLFRIEND.

"pounded you so good that he hit the *I love you* mechanism" that I relented on my ongoing stress and neurosis.

I have kept every email we have ever written to each other, now totalling 127, and when I should be filing invoices at Woodchuck I often read through them to remind myself that you actually like me. I have also saved receipts, movie ticket stubs, motel matchbooks and the scorecard from the time we tied at dinosaur minigolf.

I actually like flowers. I don't actually believe Valentine's Day to be a "commercialized manipulation of human partnerships," nor do I believe "those who participate are unimaginative tools of the corporate regime who are living a pre-constructed lie."

If I could punch any of your ex-girlfriends in the face without repercussions I would. And no, I do not think it is nice that one of them bought you an expensive Christmas and/or birthday present. And I am not actually trying to be her friend.

I am trying to be your cool girlfriend.

TWENTY

What I never told Ben was that before we went to the clinic to-gether to *get it taken care of* I picked out names.

Even after we *got it taken care of* I continued to pick out names. I wrote all of them in neat columns in a steno pad I stole from work. I kept the list in the middle of my kitchen table and added to it every time a new name came to me. That notebook became a little masochistic reminder, a tidy place to mourn, despite my hardened exterior.

Abigail
Addison
Amanda
Bailey
Becky
Bella

I didn't want Ben to be involved. I wanted Ben to go away.

Felix
Finnegan
Hailey
Hillary

Before I had it *taken care of,* Olive left me the disemboweled body of a grey mouse on the bathroom floor. She looked up at me and meowed loudly, so proud of what she had done. I picked up the corpse with a grocery bag and tossed it into the dumpster behind my apartment building.

It wasn't that I regretted the decision, it was that I wished it could have been *possible.*

Sabrina
Sadie
Tara
Tori

The morning I had it *taken care of* my ever-increasing list of baby names exceeded one hundred possible choices.

By that afternoon there were no more choices.

TWENTY-ONE

Ben was not as perfect as Adrian and the rest of my friends assumed. At times he was a mess. Although outwardly, with my panic attacks and hypochondriac pain, it appeared that he was taking care of me, there were always those moments where I was forced to throw him in a cold shower after he got too drunk at a gig, times when I had to pull him up off the bathroom floor when he was passed out in his own puke.

It's surprising, I know, but the beauty of what goes on behind closed doors is that very private vulnerability that happens when you've had way too much to drink.

One night Ben came home from the bar and decided he wanted to eat a chicken leg. Driven by this intense, misguided temptation, he opened the freezer, took out an entire chicken, pried a single leg from the rock hard frozen bird with a butcher knife, threw the mangled limb into in a sauce pot full of cold water, and put it on the stove to boil. Twenty minutes later, after a failed attempt to eat the still partially frozen leg, he shoved the entire pot in the fridge, packed a slice of stale Wonder Bread in his mouth and went to bed.

The pot, with the chicken leg still floating in it, remained in his fridge for weeks.

Not one of the three boys who lived in the house felt the need to remove the undercooked meat from its shelf above the cheese. For weeks I would see it crammed in the back of the packed fridge when I pulled out a beer or got some milk for my tea. I was trying to be a cool girlfriend, which didn't include critiquing Ben's ability to clean up after himself. Because of that, I simply stared at the decaying bird limb and felt powerless to say anything.

One night, after a particularly heated argument about how miserable and pathetic I had become, Ben stormed out of the house and I took that opportunity to do away with the decaying chicken leg once and for all. I took that pot from the fridge and decided to hide it in Ben's bed before I stormed off into the night.

Later that night I received a phone call from Ben that began with a sincere apology and ended with, "Did you give Bill anything to eat? He's not looking so good. And why is there an empty sauce pot in my bed?"

Bill ended up at the vet and after a course of antibiotics became suspicious of any food I offered him. I couldn't even get him to lick food remnants from my fingers after snacking.

Staring at the sick dog sprawled out on the living room floor the next day, I knew that was the beginning of the end.

TWENTY-TWO

Break ups always begin with a vague feeling of irritation. This little itch you feel the need to scratch with snarky comments and eye-rolling.

I'm irritated you forgot to pick up cream for the coffee.

I'm irritated that you broke my favourite mug.

I'm irritated that you forgot to tell me we were having dinner with your parents on Sunday.

You used to hold hands. You used to have sex four and a half times a week. You used to call each other for no reason.

Now you're irritated because he looked at you wrong.

"*What?*" you say.

Before you know it, you go out for Chinese food and he's ordering jelly fish salad and preserved pork just to piss you off. He asks you if you want green beans even though he knows you don't like green beans, and when you remind him he says, "What kind of fucking person doesn't like green beans?"

Conversation highlights include:

"You look weird in that dress."

"You used to love this dress."

"I'm evolving. Now I hate it."

"How is that even possible?"

"What, I'm not allowed to change my mind?"

"For fuck's sake, Ben. Why don't you just have *yet another* drink and shut up?"

"Oh yes, another drink. Better to tolerate you with, my dear." (Raises glass in a mock toast.)

When the bill comes he no longer reaches for the cheque, which is particularly irritating given how much you both now drink at dinner in order to tolerate each other.

I'M IRRITATED YOU FORGOT TO PICK
UP CREAM FOR THE COFFEE.

I'M IRRITATED THAT YOU BROKE
MY FAVOURITE MUG.

I'M IRRITATED THAT YOU FORGOT
TO TELL ME WE WERE HAVING
DINNER WITH YOUR PARENTS
ON SUNDAY.

TWENTY-THREE

Our break up had been coming for weeks, much like a pending appointment for invasive dental surgery that you ignore on the calendar until it arrives. It always seems so far away and then suddenly it's here, and the dreaded drilling begins.

What began with a sauce pot hidden in his bed evolved into constantly walking the edge of an argument.

Eventually Ben and I turned into one of those awful couples that you really just don't want to invite over for dinner anymore. The kind of couple that bickers without restraint or shame, making humiliating each other publicly an art form—a competitive sport that embarrasses everyone but themselves. The kind of couple where every "yes dear" is dripping with vile sarcasm and every conversation evolves into an argument. The kind of couple where he'll call her a bitch and she'll throw a drink at him before the night is over.

In our final days Ben got drunk more often and I got high more often, and it got to the point where all the time we spent together was simply time spent watching *Battlestar Galactica* and tolerating each other via intoxicants. Ben would fall asleep on the couch to avoid sharing a bed with me, and while he slept and snored I would stare at him with utter disgust.

Even Bill knew it was over. Whenever I came over he would hide in the bathroom for fear of fighting. If Bill did manage to tolerate being in the same room as us when we were arguing, he would obsessively clean himself to the point where his fur began to fall out in patches. His pathetic, partially bald appearance became a marker for how well our relationship was doing at any given moment.

The final day for Ben and I came when we had a twenty-minute telephone conversation during which he told me I was "such a constant downer" and I told him he was "childish."

"Marnie, I just can't."

"Fine. Then don't."

And I hung up the phone. That was it. I was amazed our relationship could end so unceremoniously.

I think subconsciously we both knew the holiday season would be intolerable if we stayed together. Attempting to conceal our growing distaste for each other from our families over turkey and stuffing was certainly a horrific possibility. Best to cut and run before I threw a drink at Ben in front of Aunt Jill and Cousin Bob.

Just over a year and ten months after Ben threw up on the sidewalk outside the bar and told me he'd love to go home with me, it was over.

Ben and I didn't speak to each other for a couple of months after he left me. Dropped me. Disposed of me. It was much easier to think about it in those terms because then I got to be the victim.

Now it was all one apple, one onion and one small container of creamer. It was whisky and cigarettes. It was quiet.

After that final conversation I quickly decided I didn't want to hear Ben's voice or see Ben's face ever again. I spent my days missing the quality time I had spent with Bill, the mastiff, at the Trinity Bellwoods dog park. Some days I would go there and just watch the dogs wrestle and run. The other dog owners would eye me sympathetically as I sat on a picnic table, chain smoking.

The reality was that sadly, Ben was right: I was a constant downer—and with him gone it just got worse. He left and I had much more room to be endlessly miserable. There was no one around to keep my overdramatic nature in check, and when given free reign to indulge, my misery was out of control.

TWENTY-FOUR

I think at some point the fear of dying alone outweighs the fear of fucking the same person for the rest of your life.

TWENTY-FIVE

Sometimes I considered the idea that I actually wanted to be as pathetic as I managed to become after Ben left. It was empowered patheticness really. His departure had merely provided me with the best kind of excuse to become completely useless.

The first thing I did post-break up was watch a lot of television. When I was deep in the stereotypical "shuffle around the apartment in your pyjamas" phase, the television was always on; it was my brand new flickering friend who never shut up, keeping me company all day long. Brenda and Brandon Walsh, The Seavers, The Keatons, Tootie, Blair, Nathalie and Jo—all of them did a wonderful job of taking my mind off things.

When Ben and I were still together he wouldn't let me get cable—he self-righteously claimed it would make me "unproductive." I always thought that sentiment was hilarious given that I didn't really ever have anything to do. The only thing I did was spend time with him, so maybe three-hundred cable channels would have been just the thing to salvage our relationship. If I could have watched reruns of *90210* I wouldn't have become so dependent on him for entertainment.

Creative people tend to forget that the rest of us have absolutely nothing to do when we're not earning money. They don't realize that the lesbian contestant on *America's Next Top Model* is as about as interesting as it gets for those of us who don't have a "calling."

So when Ben left me, I began to resent the fact that he had enough power over my life to dictate my viewing habits. I immediately called the cable guy and got the entire package. Hundreds and hundreds of channels that promised I would never be alone again. That I would never be let down. That there would always be someone there.

I had to fight not to hug the cable guy after he'd finished installing it. Thanks to him there would always an episode of the many incarnations of *CSI* on, always a moment to observe the unending sexual tension between Gil Grissom and Sarah Sidle as they hovered over a dismembered corpse together, always a chance to see Lieutenant Horatio Caine sneer at a Miami drug lord from behind his reflective sunglasses.

Because of the size of my apartment, I could turn the television in such a way that it was visible from my bed, perfect for the days I decided it wasn't worth getting up. The television and a bottle of Jim Beam whisky were the two most reliable things in my life during that time.

In my tattered pink bathrobe and bunny-print pyjamas, I would park myself on the couch and not get up for days. My coffee table would be cluttered with whisky tumblers and an ashtray full of cigarette butts while I lovingly clutched my universal remote. I came to learn the names of every actor in prime time, had an in-depth knowledge of who each of them was dating, what other things they had been in, how their career was doing in general. I was so painfully aware of the meaningless details about the world because I was completely incapable of tolerating anything real.

My favourite shows of all were the kind of vapid, entertainment gossip updates that people tend to watch when they're mentally ill. I couldn't bear watching the six o'clock news because the inarguably horrific nature of the world just made the potential plan of one day going outside that much farther away. Entertainment news was light, fluffy and innocuous enough that it at least presented a vague invitation to go outside, if only to shop for Manolo Blahniks or to buy a new Kate Spade purse.

Because of the waxy, painted faces of Ben Mulroney and Mary Hart, I became consumed with tracking the downfalls of pretty, young starlets. Blondes, brunettes, and redheads—so many of them barely out of their twenties, falling apart in beautiful, theatrical, and very public performances. Hobbling around in their Christian Louboutin Shoes, flashing their underpants (or lack of underpants) while stumbling out of SUVs, getting DUIs while careening home from a debauched Hollywood shindig—all while being chased by the constant glare of flashbulbs. Their drama, conveniently, replaced my own.

It was inspiring. I wanted the courage to acquire a drug habit or shave off all my hair.

Because I had researched the Internet so thoroughly on my own brand of insanity (and myriad potential diagnoses) I fancied myself an expert on what they were all going through.

Post traumatic stress disorder
Post-partum depression
Anxiety disorder
Manic depression
Schizophrenia
Narcissism
Loneliness
Boredom

I was too secluded and insignificant to create a fantastic, self-destructive crisis circus all around me, but I relished in watching beautiful girls go on coke binges, talk to the paparazzi nonsensically in put-on accents, and fuck anyone who offered. I was both amused and disturbed—obsessed—as I watched them strip down to their underwear for an impromptu swim in the Pacific Ocean, or claim "these pants aren't mine" when accused of drug possession by the arresting officer. I cheered as they checked into rehab and shook my head sadly when they left early.

In some strange way, their meltdowns seemed to prevent my own. The more I worried about their problems the less I had to worry about my own, which allowed me to teeter on the edge of an inevitable collapse for a short time.

POST TRAUMATIC STRESS DISORDER

POST-PARTUM DEPRESSION

ANXIETY DISORDER

MANIC DEPRESSION

SCHIZOPHRENIA

NARCISSISM

LONELINESS

BOREDOM

TWENTY-SIX

After Ben and I broke up I was coerced into buying a $169 silk cocktail dress when I ran into Beatrice, a former friend from art school that I hadn't seen in over five years. She was flustered, working in the dreaded entrapment of fashion retail during the Christmas rush.

That cliché of art school to retail.

"Oh god," she said when she spotted me lingering around the change rooms. "I'm having the fucking worst day and of course now I have to run into you and have you explain how successful and happy you are."

Now I have to lie and pretend how successful and happy I am.

She exhaled a noisy sigh while heaving a pile of rejected dresses onto a rack. I immediately wished I was wearing make-up or at least that I had bothered to brush my hair. I immediately wished I could truthfully tell her I was successful and happy.

"I'm just working here while I try to figure out what I'm going to do with my life," she said, trying to fake her own embarrassment. From what I could recall, Beatrice was never a girl who was embarrassed about anything. In my second year of university I watched her get high and make out with two guys at the same time at a house party full or art students.

Beatrice looked immaculate—beautiful white-blonde hair tied up tidily in an artful twist, pale alabaster skin and bright blue eyes, with an impossibly perfect pair of fire-engine-red lips. Wherever Beatrice perceived she had failed career-wise, she had certainly redeemed herself via her ability to put herself together. She was actually wearing a pantsuit. I didn't know a single person under the age of thirty-five who owned a pantsuit.

After some prodding I told her that I had (had) an office job that I hated, that I was single, that I was seeking a "versatile dress" for a "party-packed holiday season" ahead. Those were the only details I could invent on the spot that made my life seem vaguely intriguing.

I did not tell Beatrice that I was perfecting the life of a recluse and that it had been very difficult changing out of the same pair of rank pyjamas I had been wearing for a week.

"Oh, I'll pick out something fucking fantastic for you," she said gleefully, smoothing her already smooth blonde hair against her head. Another thing I suddenly remembered about Beatrice: her liberal use of profanity.

"Shit. Let me dress you up."

I was coerced because I was vulnerable. My ability to leave the apartment post-break up with Ben was severely limited. The idea of seeing someone I knew was devastating, especially someone I needed to impress. I was incapable of impressing anyone.

I submitted to the torture of her selecting dresses for me because fighting her off would have been slightly more difficult. But only slightly.

Beatrice proceeded to pick out a variety of garish, sparkly spangled dresses of varying colours and degrees of hilarity. I painfully pulled them on over my mismatched bra and underpants in the cramped discomfort of the change room, constantly aware of the fact that the curtain was doing a poor job of concealing me from the other customers. Beatrice watched sadistically as I sweated, awkwardly modelling every obnoxious garment for her as she either cooed her delight or crinkled her upturned nose in disgust.

Halfway through the performance she passive aggressively commented that from what she could recall, "dressing up" was

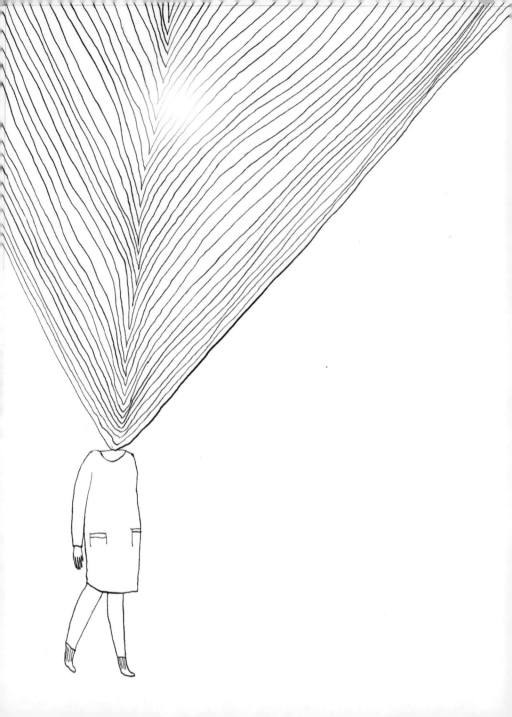

always out of my "comfort zone," motioning to my pile of beige and brown cotton clothes that lay in a pathetic mass on the floor of the change room.

From what I could recall, Beatrice was a self-righteous bitch, but I kept that to myself.

"You know Marnie, you'd be really fucking pretty if—"

I came to realize that the more ridiculous the dress looked on me, the more likely she was to look triumphant and inform me that I looked "fucking fantastic." The adoration was suspect. I began to sweat profusely out of increasing anxiety. An hour later I was exhausted and starting to smell, tired of standing in front of a full length mirror in an absurd party dress and white tube socks with holes in the toes. Beatrice had finally managed to convince me to buy a purple and brown, silk sack dress on what little credit I had left.

"Much better than those fucking old man sweaters you used to always wear at school," she stated when I studied myself apathetically in the mirror. I knew the hefty price tag was the fee allowing me to finally leave.

She carried my purchase to the cashier, letting her know with a telling smile that she had been the one "helping me."

"It was so fucking great to see you, Marnie. We should really keep in touch," she said, without offering her phone number.

The cashier, who was wearing make-up and not wearing an old man sweater, informed me the dress was final sale.

As suspected, I never wore that dress to any holiday parties, or anywhere else. Instead I put it on to eat ice cream and watch television with the cat.

Sometimes I wished Ben could have seen me in it, if only so I could have heard his laugh again.

TWENTY-SEVEN

As if sensing my personal disaster from afar, my mother calls me. The shrill ring of the phone startles me while I'm staring blankly into the fridge, attempting to choose something to cook for breakfast on a Saturday morning. Her and my father are early risers, the way older people always seem to be, and while I'm in my pyjamas, mumbling my hello into the phone, I can visualize her multi-tasking, cleaning up their breakfast while she's talking to me on the big, avocado coloured kitchen phone.

Her and my father have lived together in a suburban house in Scarborough for over thirty years. When my sister and I left home they took on a team of animals rescued from their local shelter. At last count there were three dogs and four cats, meaning that the house always smells like a barnyard when I go home to visit.

My parents are blissfully in love to the point where it kind of makes me physically ill. It certainly contributes to me being mentally ill. While all the other kids in my elementary school were suffering the ill-effects of their parents splitting up, I would experience the nausea associated with catching your folks making out in the laundry room. People often discuss the ramifications of divorce on small children, but they never mention how emotionally scarring having parents in love can be. The pressure is immense.

"Marianne. How are you?" My mother is the only person in my life who consistently calls me *Marianne*. Only people that really love me call me *Marianne*.

"You know. Alive."

I make the decision to poach an egg as a solution to my raging whisky hangover, the result of yet another post-break up evening of self-loathing. My lungs feel like they're full of silt thanks to the pack of cigarettes I smoked yesterday, and I cover the phone as I cough up whatever blackness is destroying me. Olive is erratically chasing what seems to be imaginary spiders across the linoleum and I almost trip over her while I take the two steps from the fridge to the stove. I inspect a loaf of rye bread that has just crossed the line into stale. I decide to scrape off some mould and eat it anyway.

"Have you been to visit your grandmother lately?" she asks. She always asks me this. I am convinced that it is out of guilt, as she rarely visits her own mother except on special occasions.

"I've been meaning to," I lie. "How's Cynthia?"

"She's doing so well. She joined the rowing team."

"Of course she did."

"What does that mean?"

It means that Cynthia's not always drunk and lonely, hiding from the world while slowly going insane. She's not considering cutting herself off completely from the rest of society. It means she's not developing an unhealthy dependence on E-Talk Daily.

"Marianne," my mother says in her trademark *I'm desperately trying to be sensitive* voice, "you should really get out more. Make some new friends. Go out with the girls in the office."

I had never once mentioned a single girl at the office to my mother. In fact, while I fill a saucepan with water and pop a piece of rye toast in the toaster, I realize that there weren't ever any girls in the Woodchuck office.

"How's Ben?" she asked when her critique of my social life was faced with silence.

"Ben left me." Saying it out loud felt surreal.

It appeared now that the cat had managed to catch something, which she was now smacking around in her mouth noisily. On the other end of the phone my mother had started crying—quietly at first, and then her sniffles evolved into full-blown heaving. The toast popped up—it was burnt on one side.

"Oh Marnie, I'm terrified. I'm terrified that you're going to end up alone for the rest of your life. You know, your sister met that lovely boy in her political science class and they're already talking about marriage."

I watched as Olive swallowed her catch in an exaggerated gulp.

"Imagine how I feel, Mom."

TWENTY-EIGHT

The night I lost Olive was the night I finally realized why Ben left me.

The fire alarm in my apartment building went off at 2:26 a.m. and I remember blinking at the clock when I was jolted from sleep. I was wearing a Led Zeppelin t-shirt and a pair of Ben's oversized plaid flannel pyjamas. I pulled on my parka and took the time to brush my hair and clumsily apply pressed powder to my puffy face before I joined the other tenants on the snow-covered lawn.

While we were waiting for the fire truck to arrive, I eyed the middle-aged woman from 4B. She was wearing a pink shower cap on her head and clutching a ten-pound floppy eared bunny rabbit in the folds of her floral print bathrobe.

Standing there in the freezing cold, feeling sorry for her and her only companion, I suddenly realized I forgotten Olive in the potential blazing inferno upstairs.

How does one forget one's only roommate when a fire alarm goes off in the middle of the night?

Now that Ben was gone, Olive was the only living thing that depended on me for anything. Her needs consisted only of a couple of tins of putrid cat food and a clean litter box and water dish. I suppose I had haphazardly adopted her years ago because I selfishly needed something to rely on me, her lack of a tail made her look needy and incomplete, and I was sure she would love me unconditionally. But she was a cat so she didn't. In fact lately I was sure she was growing to resent me.

She had good reason. In the face of a fire that threatened to engulf the four-story building I lived in, it was apparently easy for me to abandon her. I hadn't thought twice about trotting out to the lawn and leaving her behind to cower under the bed, in terror of a shrill, shrieking bell.

Under the bed, amongst the dust bunnies and discarded candy wrappers, was where I found her after I disregarded the other tenants' warnings to stay safely outside. She glared at me

disapprovingly and meowed angrily as I got down on all fours and attempted to coerce her out of hiding with a broom. After a minute of calling her name she darted past me and out the open front door.

It was later reported through the apartment building rumour mill that a drunk tenant had made an attempt to fry up some bacon after returning from the bar, and the combination of one too many vodka shots and bacon grease was the reason we were all jolted from sleep in the wee hours of a Thursday morning. He was appropriately chastised by management and his fellow apartment dwellers in the days that followed, but Olive never returned from her hasty exit out a propped open fire escape door. I was eyed sympathetically as I hung photocopies of her picture in the laundry room in the days that followed, but in my heart I knew she was better off without me.

While I was capable of being relied on for keeping my complexion and hair looking their best during an anticipated fire-related tragedy, I was incapable of having anyone, not even a shelter cat with a handful of needs, rely on me for anything else.

No wonder I am lonely, inconsequential.

No wonder Ben left me.

TWENTY-NINE

A few months after he and I broke up—just after I quit my job and just before I made the decision to have everything I could ever want or need delivered directly to my apartment—I was at Shoppers Drug Mart buying acne cream and tampons and I ran into Ben. He was with a beautiful red-headed girl in a lemon yellow vintage dress with an electric blue scarf on her head. She was at least a foot taller than I was, and, unlike me, not wearing the clothes she slept in last night. He didn't introduce me to her.

"Ben," I said, obviously startled. I could feel my face getting pink.

"Marnie," he said.

"I'm going to go get that, um, thing we need," the amazonian redhead said, quickly departing to (horrifyingly) the prophylactic aisle. Her quick departure gave her the appearance of being understanding and intuitive.

I desperately wanted to punch her in her understanding and intuitive face.

I stood there frozen for a moment, clutching my acne cream and econo-size box of super-absorbent tampons, and took in Ben's signature smell. It was basically the same as when we had shared a bed, but a little cleaner, a little more Irish Spring and a little less body odour. I felt a chill as the realization hit me that he'd likely made deliberate hygienic efforts to impress the redhead. The redhead who I was sure was right now picking out condoms "for her pleasure."

"How have you been?" he asked, making a slight attempt to smile.

"Really good," I lied.

"You look great," he lied.

I knew how I looked. I knew that I had stopped caring about how I looked weeks ago. I was sure the redhead in the headscarf was wearing expensive underwear and that her bra matched that underwear.

There was a long, excruciating pause. Then, out of nowhere, Ben reached out and delicately touched my cheek, much like he had done that first time we'd met, just before he threw up on the sidewalk.

"I miss you, Marianne."

The words were enough for me to drop the acne cream and the tampons. I hated him for saying something so manipulative.

"No you don't," I said.

"Then come back to me, Ben," I wanted to say.

While I bent down to retrieve my embarrassing items Ben made some random excuse relating to his need to leave. He then retrieved his understanding and intuitive redhead in the fancy underwear and bee-lined for the exit without purchasing that "thing" they needed.

Standing there, abandoned and bewildered, I went back to missing Bill, the mastiff, and wishing Ben (and now the redhead) dead.

Panic: characterized by a sudden rush of intense fear that is accompanied by a number of intense physical sensations.
It is important to remember that you are not dying.
That this will pass.
That it's all in your head.
That it was all, always, in your head.

Symptoms include:

Rapid heartbeat, pounding heart or palpitations
Sweating
Shaking visibly or inside
Choking sensations or lump in the throat
Smothering or shortness of breath sensations
Chest pain or discomfort
Nausea, bloating, indigestion or abdominal discomfort
Dizziness or unsteadiness
Light-headedness
Fear of losing control or going crazy
Paresthesia (numbness or tingling sensations) in face,
extremities or body
Chills or hot flushes
Derealization or feeling unreal
Depersonalisation or feeling like you don't exist

My name is Marnie and I'm invisible.

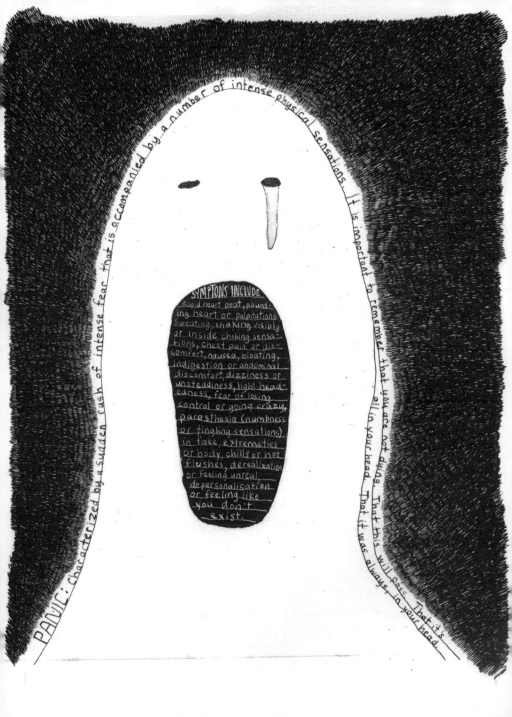

PANIC: Characterized by a sudden rush of intense fear that is accompanied by a number of intense physical sensations. It is important to remember that you are not dying, all in your head. That this will pass. That it's always in your head.

SYMPTONS INCLUDE
Rapid heart beat, pounding heart or palpitations, sweating, shaking visibly or inside, choking sensations, chest pain or discomfort, nausea, bloating, indigestion or abdominal discomfort, dizziness or unsteddiness, light headedness, fear of losing control or going crazy, paresthesia (numbness or tingling sensations) in face, extremeties or body, chills or hot flushes, derealization or feeling unreal, depersonalisation or feeling like you don't exist.

MY NAME IS MARNIE AND I'M INVISIBLE.

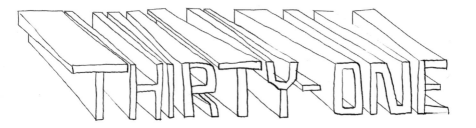

THIRTY-ONE

It was the panic attacks that drove me permanently inside.

After a few weeks of indulgently moping around town on account of my recent singularity, I came out of my drunken, unshowered fog only to be struck down by an impending sense of doom and my very real physical reaction to it.

A few isolated incidents where I assumed I was having a heart attack turned into an ever-present feeling that I could keel over at any moment. It took very little time for the Internet to let me know I was suffering from anxiety, but by then I was convinced that going outside was a terrible idea. It was no surprise that my pervasive hypochondria would eventually evolve into house-bound anxiety. As much as my logic and reason knew it was all in my head, I nevertheless retreated inside and stayed there.

Within a mere few weeks I had developed a fear of open spaces and a fear of enclosed ones. I had trouble swallowing, trouble focusing, trouble leaving the house. I did things like vomit before meeting people for drinks and when I was there I would tell my friends that, "alcohol makes me feel better."

I was afraid to take the subway, afraid to eat at restaurants, afraid to enter bookstores.

I was completely obsessed with tragedy. I was sure it was around every corner, and I waited for it, readied for it in a way I never had before. It was true that losing him had made me afraid of any future disasters, but now that he was gone I also longed for it. Loved it. It confirmed that I was still alive.

I collected memoirs of tragic, filmic lives: Dorothy Dandridge, Jayne Mansfield, Marilyn Monroe, Sharon Tate, Natalie Wood.

I watched television shows about hospitals, prisons and true crime, and carefully selected movies where the protagonist would meet a tragic end. I yearned for violence—every incarnation of *Law and Order* and *CSI* was delivered to me by the mailman via my online rental account.

I would search the Internet endlessly for possible ailments,

I COLLECTED MEMOIRS OF TRAGIC, FILMIC LIVES: DOROTHY DANDRIDGE, JAYNE MANSFIELD, MARILYN MONROE, SHARON TATE, NATALIE WOOD.

particularly those that included shocking, graphic photos of ill-nesses I had never before even considered.

I would pull out the obituaries on Saturdays and search for people who died before their time, circling the photos of their smiling faces with a red marker while casually sipping a cup of Jasmine tea. Finding someone listed there who was dead in their twenties was a morbid victory, proving that my fear of the statisti-cally improbable was completely warranted.

After I was done with the obituaries I would move on to the horoscopes, looking to mine to try to validate my sense of im-pending doom.

When I was done I would read Ben's, and hope the doom was his instead.

At first I would go for drinks with friends on weekends and while tipping back their pints they would say things like, "don't be so dramatic, Marnie." Or, "snap out of it, Marnie." They were all intent on healing me, fixing me, or setting me up with some-one new.

To remedy this situation I simply stopped going for drinks with friends on weekends.

What they all didn't understand was that being dramatic was the one thing that kept me going. Once Ben was gone, the cre-ation of drama was the only thing that seemed to validate that I was still alive. Without Ben to make me interesting, I was fading away, closer and closer to invisible with each passing day. With-out the creation of drama, I was numb. Empty.

Sometimes when someone's heart is broken they become ob-sessed with self-destruction, drinking and smoking and sweating the pain away with strangers. They stand on the bar at 1 a.m. while they tip back shooters, singing and kissing and inevitably crying because the song on the jukebox relentlessly reminds them about what they lost. They see no reason for living any-more and they make that abundantly clear to everyone around them. That kind of masochism simply wasn't the case with me. When Ben left me I became consumed with an obsessive need for self-preservation, determined to protect myself from any further rejection or damage. It was as if there had been a sudden alien invasion or a nuclear war and I was forced to seal myself inside my apartment, duct taping the doors and tin foiling the windows. My fear was that something unknown outside would harm me. I was afraid of anything new.

I started to get all of my groceries delivered, stockpiling instant soups, canned goods and bottled water. The idea of conversing with other people became so unappealing that I began buying things off the Internet so I wouldn't ever have to enter a store and talk to a shop clerk. I would spend endless hours on eBay, flag-ging objects of desire, vintage outfits to wear to parties I would never attend and delicate objets d'art to decorate my increasingly crowded abode.

To avoid starving I started taking on a strange series of free-lance jobs that didn't require me to leave the house for meetings and appointments. The agency called it "telecommuting," which

I could only think was a generous way to describe work for lazy or, in my case, insane members of the workforce. I made strange telemarketing calls and stuffed envelopes—anything to prevent me from going outside.

To relax, I had multiple baths a day. Sometimes four or five. Until one day it occurred to me I could die in the bathtub and be found there, naked, purple and bloated, many days later. After that I began having very short showers, enveloped in debilitating full- blown panic while I attempted to bathe in under a minute.

Being confined to the four walls of my studio apartment meant nothing could ever penetrate me. I was completely protected from harm, even instructing the UPS man to leave the latest delivery of tragic memoirs from Amazon outside my door.

The hardest part about disappearing was the undeniable knowledge that no one really missed me or even noticed I was gone. It's a fact that when you stop making phone calls, you stop receiving them. No one sought me out when I was enclosed in my five hundred square foot shell and that seemed to suit me fine, but there was, admittedly, an even more intense sense of meaninglessness to my life. I suppose the difference was that I had finally surrendered to it.

While watching crime scene investigation shows, I pondered how long it would take for someone to find me if I dropped dead while making my macaroni and cheese for dinner.

THIRTY-TWO

When the winter came, Marnie started to visit more often. She didn't tell me why, she just started appearing at my door every few days, requesting tea and company.

Of course I knew why.

I know it's selfish, but I was glad the boy was gone. She deserved better and I would have told her so if she'd ever brought it up. I knew that better would never be me, but I was happy to stand in for the brief time I was useful.

I've always tried to be a good man. I care about tragedies that occur in non-English speaking countries.

I am appropriately outraged when dogs and babies have to be rescued from overheated cars in July.

I yearn to reduce my carbon-footprint, despite the fact that I'm not entirely sure what that means.

I buy locally, floss occasionally, take vitamins, and try to drink tea instead of coffee.

Water instead of wine.

Salad instead of steak.

I read the newspaper.

I donate thirty-five dollars a year to the Toronto Humane Society.

Sometimes I even moisturize.

But it's Marnie that really makes me feel like a good man.

There are days when I wonder if I'll ever be in love again.

There are days that I really don't care if I'm ever in love again.

Because of Marnie, I have all the love I need.

I've always liked books better than people. Not only are they safer and smarter, they're certainly more interesting. Marnie's the only person that I ever wanted to share anything with; books, tea, moments, secrets, feelings, love.

There are days when, because of her, I feel everything—I am so alive and aware.

And then there are days when I close the bathroom door, sit on the toilet and cry because there's too many things that I need to care about, too many things I need to feel.

Marnie makes me feel like a good man.

Marnie makes me glad I moisturize.

THIRTY-THREE

Adrian shows up at my door one Sunday afternoon and casually offers me a stockpile of Xanax and Atavan.

I hug him and burst into tears.

I am a train wreck. A caricature. A stereotype. Bat-shit crazy.

THIRTY-FOUR

When I wasn't buying books on Amazon or bidding on vintage dresses on eBay, I was reading the missed connections posts on Craigslist. I hungered for those first naïve moments of potential love recorded by stupid people. Their belief in the impossible cheered me, and I tracked their postings and responses daily in the hope of finding an optimism that had left me.

I fantasized about each of them meeting, despite the fact that Toronto was a city of 2.48 million people and a poorly written paragraph was an unlikely way to get in touch.

-You are the most beautiful woman I've ever seen. I was turning left from Britannia onto Queen. We looked at each other, You are breathtaking. You were driving a beige Corolla.
You winked, or was it something in your eye? Did we a share a moment?
-I was at the intersection of Church and Richmond, around 9:30 p.m. and asked you for the time. I thought you were a cutie. Coffee?
-You are the incredibly beautiful brunette that works at Shoppers Drug Mart at Dovercourt & Bloor. Your pen ran out of ink yesterday when I was signing my Visa slip. I've always wanted to talk to you but it just never seems right. I saw you tonight working the beauty department desk when I was walking home. I'd love to take you out for dinner and drinks.

And then I found this:

-You have missed a connection with your common sense if you really think I don't actually know what's going on.
Just thought you should know that while you're cheating on me with her I'm making plans to leave you for good. I hope the slut is worth it.

Thanks to that, I lost whatever optimism I had left.

The immediacy of modern technology was also the reason I was incapable of avoiding the memory of Ben. I was googling him incessantly. I set up Google alerts to ensure I didn't miss a single life event. I knew exactly when his band was playing, and the night of each gig I resisted the urge to show up. Once I even got completely dressed (right down to my winter coat and boots) to attend a show he was playing at The Cameron House, only to instead end up on my couch eating Swiss Chalet takeout, feeling sorry for myself.

The worst and most embarrassing of all my cyber-stalking related to obsessively watching Ben's collection of social networking sites. Every morning when I woke up I would sit down at my kitchen table with my laptop and a cup of tea and check to see if Ben had added any new girls to his ever-increasing roster of friends. When he did, I would look at his events calendar and try to track where he might have met them.

Ben is attending Sarah's twenty-second birthday party.
Ben is attending Emily's erotic poetry reading.
Ben is attending the gallery opening of Daria's nude self-portraits.

There were always new girls, always young and pretty, always younger and prettier than me. I would study their profiles to see what they were like, scrutinize their relationship status, their interests, their favourite bands and books.

Sydney's favourite books: The Diaries of Anaïs Nin, The Story of O, The Collected Poetry of William Blake, *anything by Tolstoy.*
Chelsey's favourite books: She Came to Stay *by Simone de Beauvoir*

Heather's favourite musicians: Leonard Cohen, Nico, Nick Drake, Elliott Smith, Donovan.
Danielle' favourite musicians: The Smiths.

All of these beautiful girls would invite Ben to join their groups, groups that pretentious, misguided twenty-somethings join, like "Free Tibet" and "Darfur Activists."
Because they truly believe that joining an online group is an effective method to liberate a people.

Monique has joined the group "Bad Grammar is Just Wrong"
Linda is a fan of McSweeney's

I combatted all of my hatred and jealousy by mocking their various profile pictures. They were always the same; pictures they took of themselves in their polka-dotted and pink heart-printed underpants—vain girls who loved their own reflections, each trying to be subtle while faux kissing the camera.
If all these new girls checked out my profile, with my bland profile picture—a vacation photo of Ben and me in Niagara Falls, a picture I had cropped him out of—I could imagine the conversations he had with them.
"Yah, I dated this girl named Marnie. She was a real downer. Kind of crazy."

Marnie's activities: hating you.
Marnie's interests: hiding from everyone.
I looked at their saccharine, smiling, digital kissy-faces and I fucking detested them all.

THIRTY-FIVE

One of many humiliating break up experiences:

Calling my cell phone provider to finally cancel our "couples plan" and having the teenage customer service representative fight to retain me as a customer.

"Maybe you'll get back together? Or maybe you have someone else you can use the plan with?"

"No."

"Well, don't worry. I'm sure you'll find someone soon."

"You know what? Let's just cancel the phone all together."

I am almost thirty.

    On one side of me there is that past-tense girl. That nubile girl I could have been. The one who is up on the bar, her midriff bare, dancing to rock anthems and tipping back shots while her admirers look on. People love her. People fuck her. People get her name tattooed on their forearms and never grow up to regret it. I always wanted to be that girl.

On the other side of me there are disapproving glares at baby showers and engagement parties for couples I'm not really sure why I'm friends with. There are platters of tiny sandwiches and mortgage payments and daycare and regrets.

There are people in love who feel sorry for me and invite me to dinner parties out of sympathy.

There's "Don't worry Marnie, you're really pretty. You'll find someone."

There's "When are you going to settle down, Marnie?"

But I don't want to find anyone. And I'm so settled I'm practically comatose.

There are still days that I miss Ben. Days when those sympathetic friends say, "Maybe you should call Ben and go for a drink. Talk."

About what?

I loved Ben. I know that now. I loved the way his hair always looked like he just rolled out of bed. I loved the way he used to bring me candy and pull it from his pockets like an eager child. I loved the way he'd let me eat his fortune cookie when we got Chinese take out. I loved the way he noticed and remembered everything, the way he sent me a bouquet of flowers on the one-year anniversary of the day we went to the abortion clinic and never mentioned it. The way he remembered that my Mom liked Monk's Blend Tea and that she used it to quit drinking coffee, and

the way he never drank coffee around her because he remembered that. He was thoughtful that way, and I loved him for it.
I missed all of those perfect moments with him desperately, but
being alone now felt so much safer than the vulnerability he'd
brought out in me.

THIRTY-SEVEN

One morning in early April I was retrieving the paper from outside my front door and Olive was sitting on the front-page head-
line as if she had never left.

Terrorist Organization Claims Responsibility for Blast and Olive,
sitting there on my welcome mat.

The cat looked up at me and meowed, and I dramatically burst
into tears. I did so loudly enough that Neil clicked open his door

slightly to see if I was okay. In my hysteria I chose to ignore him and he simply closed the door again.

Olive was covered in a thin film of filth and she had lost the bulk of her endearingly plump body weight, but she was certainly the same tailless cat that had bolted from my apartment during a fire alarm a few months earlier.

She trotted between my legs and through the open door, scurrying straight to where her food bowl once was. How she had managed to survive outside during the winter months and avoid Toronto Animal Services was beyond me, but I chose not to think too much about her recent experiences and simply praised her for returning to me. I told her repeatedly how sorry I was as I rummaged around in the kitchen cupboards in the hopes of sourcing some leftover cat food. In the end I decided to treat her to a tin of tuna as a reward for her belated return. She circled my feet wildly and frantically meowed as I opened the tin with a can opener.

You wouldn't have to be overly superstitious to interpret Olive's return as a clear indication that it was time for me to go back outside into the world. Although it was an impending heart attack or aneurism that had forced me to hide, the advent of springtime had already prompted a shift in me. Olive was the furry little prophet of hope and renewal that I needed for a final push out the door. If she could forgive me for my neglect and return to the apartment, I could certainly start doing my grocery shopping in public again. Although I knew the kind of social loneliness that that activity threatened, I could endure it with the knowledge that Olive was now at home waiting for me.

As soon as she was fed and then unhappily bathed in my kitchen sink, I cancelled my most recent online orders and opened all the curtains and windows. The smell of the outside world filled the apartment with a sickly, sweet optimism that I forced myself to adjust to.

Olive immediately found a patch of sunlight on the couch to fall asleep in and I decided to go outside. I scheduled an afternoon beer with Adrian via email because I was now without a phone. It took only a few minutes for him to email me back.

"Is it because you need more Valium?" was how he responded.

I opened the front door of the apartment and kicked aside the most recent pile of packages that had been left for me.

Neil was standing outside, removing his rain boots before going into his apartment. His door was slightly open and I could see the walls and walls of built-in shelving that he installed himself—an endless floor to ceiling series of books, each shelf completely jam packed. When the books couldn't find a home on a shelf they spilled out into little piles on the floor, a series of tiny tables of books that held tea cups and empty glasses. It looked tempting and safe inside.

"Morning, Marnie. I haven't seen you in a while," my neighbour lied, running his hands quickly back and forth through his greying hair. It obviously made him uncomfortable that he'd seen me crying into my sleeve earlier that day.

"No, I guess not. I've been really busy."

Busy being miserable.

"Um, do you want to come inside for a tea? I have some new books I found for you."

"Actually, I think I'm gonna go outside."

THIRTY-EIGHT

"Marnie, what happened to you? You look fucking terrible," Adrian said, pouring beer into my pint glass.

We were sitting out on a patio on Church street on what Adrian informed me was the first day warm enough to sit out on a patio. Being out in the daylight, in public, made me self-conscious about what months of recycled air and misery had done to my complexion. Not to mention my conversation skills.

"Well, welcome back to the world anyway. You've been missed," he said. "You know, I saw Ben the other day with that freak he's been seeing. So unattractive."

"Don't lie, Adrian."

"Okay, she's spectacular. But I'm sure she's really, really boring."

THIRTY-NINE

One of the first things I did after Olive liberated me from my apartment was go visit my grandmother at the senior's home. It was partially out of obligation to my mother, but I really genuinely wanted to see her as a test of my new ability to leave the house and not succumb to the throes of panic.

It was her eighty-fifth birthday, so I felt the occasion was a good first excursion for me to attempt to tolerate. Truth was I had been avoiding visits with her for a while now, even before my reclusive period; the idea of being surrounded by people who were knocking on death's door did little for my pervasive hypochondria.

Besides the obvious stench of death that hung in the air at the seniors home, there was another reason I had been avoiding grandma. It was one of the many things Ben and I did together. I had been avoiding reading comic books, eating sushi, and listening to David Bowie for the same reason.

Ben used to love visiting my Grandma on the occasional Sunday afternoon. He would talk to all of the residents about their lives, yelling his endless questions while playing chess or watching *Murder She Wrote*. It was almost embarrassing how enthusiastic he was to be around all of these dying people. He would ask endlessly about "the war" and prompt stories that began with the phrase "back in my day." While he was always enthralled, I stifled a yawn and had to drag him out when it was "nap time."

My grandmother adored Ben, thought he was perfect and used to talk openly about our "big church wedding." I hadn't yet told her that Ben and I were no longer walking towards the aisle and, honestly, didn't plan to. Given that she likely only had a few years left, I didn't really see any point of letting her down.

And so, on a Sunday afternoon, I shelved my personal anxiety, dressed conservatively, and took the bus to the home with a homeopathic remedy in my pocket.

My grandmother had an April birthday and on the last day of the month every other resident who had a birthday that month

celebrated another year with her. There were twelve other octo-
genarians that were planning to wear the five-inch "It's my birthday!" buttons they distributed.

When I arrived my grandmother was in her room getting ready
for the party. She was wearing a floral print dress and a lavender
cashmere sweater with a bejeweled purple broach on it. She was
adjusting her grey pillbox hat in the mirror.

"Marnie. You're Marnie. Where's Ben?" was the first thing she
asked me when I walked into her room.

"He's sick today, Grandma. You know the rules." The lie was a
convenient one. Anyone with even the slightest cold was forbid-
den from entering the home. A minor bug could sweep through
like a plague, rendering everyone completely helpless.

Her disappointment was obvious. For the first little while
she refused to make eye contact with me while pouting into the
mirror like a child. I resisted the urge to be annoyed with her. It
was completely irrelevant to her that my anxiety meant it had
taken every iota of strength I had to get out of my bunny-print
pyjamas and board a bus.

Of course my grandmother knew nothing of my anxiety, nor
did she know that I had been trapped inside for almost three
months. She just knew it was her birthday,

I sat on the end of her single bed and watched as she applied a
bright pink coral shade of lipstick and then smoothed the front of
her sweater with her palms.

"I think I'm ready now, Marnie," she said.

FUNNY YOU SHOULD ASK, GRANDMA. BEN IS WITH HER WITH A SIX-FOOT TALL, REDHEAD. BEN IS PROBABLY HAVING TANTRIC SEX WITH HER WHILE LISTENING TO BOWIE'S LOW. BEN IS PROBABLY EVEN LETTING THE DOG WATCH. WHAT BEN IS DEFINITELY NOT DOING IS WATCHING CABLE TELEVISION. BEN IS INSTEAD REVELLING IN BEING WITH SOMEONE WHO ISN'T SUCH A CONSTANT DOWNER.

A god-awful scream, one that resembled what I imagined a terrified and tortured lamb would sound like, echoed from the other end of the wing. My grandmother ignored it in a way that suggested it happened all the time. She continued to study her appearance, occasionally applying or removing something in the hopes of improving it.

"Is Ben coming?" she asked when she was satisfied with her reflection.

I ignored her. "C'mon Grandma, let's go downstairs to the party."

I took her hand and led her into the hallway towards the only two elevators. All of the other residents on her floor were gathered around, waiting, causing a jam of walkers and wheelchairs. My grandmother was obviously impatient.

"Marnie, we have to get downstairs or I won't get a button."

"Don't worry Grandma, you'll get a button. I promise."

"Where's Ben?"

Funny you should ask, Grandma. Ben is with a six-foot tall red-head. Ben is probably having tantric sex with her while listening to David Bowie's Low. Ben is probably even letting the dog watch. What Ben is definitely not doing is watching cable television. Ben is instead revelling in being with someone who isn't such a constant downer.

The tiny elevator on my grandmother's floor only took six people at a time and the other one was out of order. It took a full twenty minutes for all thirty-five residents on the floor to make it down to the dining room. When she and I finally walked into the dining room, the seven seats at the head table, reserved for those residents with April birthdays, had already been taken. My grandmother squeezed my hand tightly when she saw that she would be forced to sit with everyone else.

"But I wanted to sit there," she said in a tiny, childlike voice.

After a brief conversation with a less than pleasant female staff member I was forced to tell my grandmother that sitting at the front was an impossibility and she would "have to wait until next year." As I said it, I realized that waiting until next year might be a lot to ask when next year wasn't guaranteed.

I ate red Jello from a plastic bowl and somehow endured watching the birthday festivities. There was something truly awful about witnessing people who had experienced more than I ever had being treated like kindergartners and spoken to in baby voices.

An hour later the ordeal was over and I escorted my Grandmother back to her room. Because she was more mobile than most we ended up beating the rush, snagging the first elevator. While we were in it, it occurred to me that maybe she didn't want to go back to her bedroom cell so quickly, that maybe hanging out in the residence's hallway was as about as exciting as it got for her lately.

As the elevator doors opened we were greeted by Shirley, the resident crazy lady, renowned for stealing objects from people's rooms and hiding them in other people's rooms.

"But I didn't hit him," she randomly told us as we pushed past her. She was wearing a pea green, shapeless housedress that looked like it hadn't been washed since its creation in 1942.

Shirley's grey hair was sticking up at every angle and she was clutching a floral-print pillow as if it were a child. She shuffled behind us in her fuzzy pink slippers, floating across the hotel-style hallway carpet to my grandmother's room while muttering a series of incomprehensible phrases.

"But I didn't hit him. I told him that he was bad, but I didn't hit him. He's a liar. He's a liar."

When Shirley attempted to follow us into the bedroom my grandmother turned to me abruptly and spat "Get her the fuck out of here."

I shut the door quickly as Shirley continued to rant, and sat down next to my grandmother on the bed.

"Did you have a nice day, Grandma?"

She looked up at me briefly and then looked away, saying nothing.

A rocking chair faced the room's only window, a window that didn't open. The view was nothing more than a concrete courtyard.

I could picture my grandmother endlessly staring into the empty yard.

While I had spent the last few months hiding away in my single room and a half, my grandmother had probably been desperate to escape hers.

"Next time, bring Ben," she said.

The spring came and Marnie stopped coming over to my apartment for talk and tea. I knew that this was a good thing that she was finally leaving the house again and tried so hard to be happy for her, but I also knew the fact that she was feeling better meant she wasn't coming over for visits any more.

I tried to keep her in my life by leaving books outside her apartment door, giving her a reason to visit when she needed to return them.

Sadly she merely left them for me—I would come home only to find a small pile of returned books on my welcome mat, with a post-it note affixed to the cover of the top book, stating, "Thanks. Looking forward to more. xo Marnie."

As soon as Marnie started looking forward to things, I knew she didn't need me anymore.

One Thursday, at two in the afternoon, the impossibly beautiful redhead that I never officially met in Shoppers Drug Mart showed up at my front door.

No one had come to visit me for months and all of a sudden there she was, wearing an emerald green mini-dress and a pair of four inch leopard print stilettos. Up close she was seemingly perfect—and apparently very drunk. She was also a full foot taller than me while balanced on her dominatrix-esque shoes.

"Where's Ben?" she spat at me, without introducing herself.

"Not here," I replied, deadpan. I was surprising myself with my bout of sudden confidence. I never had any confidence.

"You're a fucking liar," she responded. She had an accent—a British affectation that reminded me of Madonna or Gwyneth Paltrow. The kind of accent boring, pretentious people put on to make themselves seem interesting.

"No really, he's not here. I promise." My façade was wavering along with the redhead's anger.

The accusation could only mean that Ben was cheating on her. You could see it in her face. The way she simultaneously hated and wanted to hug me.

"I know he's still in love with you. I know he is," she blurted out. She was crying now, and I was impressed with how beautiful she managed to look while completely falling apart. I just got all blotchy while I balled my eyes out.

"No really, I haven't seen him in months." I reached out my hand to touch her arm but changed my mind at the last moment. I resisted the urge to feel flattered by the fact that this ethereal girl was somehow jealous of me. She wiped her nose with the sleeve of her slate grey cardigan.

"You should really get tested for Chlamydia," she said into her wrist.

And then I understood. The redhead knew that Ben was cheating on her because she knew Ben had cheated on me with her.

"What's your name?" I asked her.

"Fiona," she sniffled

"Fiona, do you want to come in for some wine?"

FOURTY-TWO

Fiona was a grad student in sexuality studies at the University of Toronto. She let me know she had an academic interest in fetish culture and then, much to my terror, proceeded to talk at length about it while seated at my kitchen table. I tried not to reveal how sick the conversation made me while I was pouring her a third glass of wine. It was hard not to imagine her interest in bondage playing out in the bed I once slept in with Ben. While she rambled on about what she called "the socio-political ramifications of in-timate power-exchange," I stared at her shoes. Her lady shoes. The kinds of shoes that girls who have really, really good sex wear. By contrast, my Birkenstocks sat sheepishly on the welcome mat like two prudish, leather lumps. I pulled my argyle knee-socks up self-consciously.

As the alcohol flowed liberally, Fiona told me how she had met Ben at a gig Clifford had played at the Horseshoe Tavern, two months before he and I had broken up. She felt the need to tell me she was wearing "the most adorable little pink dress," that she drank too many lemon drops with her girlfriends, and then "somehow ended up fucking him" in the women's bathroom.

I had never "somehow ended up fucking" anybody.

As she told me this story I remembered that I had been sick with the flu that night. I remembered that Ben had come by my apartment at around 1 a.m. to make sure I was feeling okay. That he had made me chicken soup, put a cold compress on my forehead and watched an episode of *Firefly* with me until I fell asleep.

I then remembered how disgusting the bathrooms at the Horseshoe Tavern were. The vision of him pushing her up against a bathroom stall and fucking her underneath her adorable pink dress was vividly looping in my mind.

Fiona suddenly stopped her story. "Marnie, are you all right?" she asked me. Evidently the nausea was apparent on my face.

It wasn't long before Fiona and I finished the wine and moved on to the whisky. (While I had made a conscious attempt to start leaving the house again, I certainly hadn't ended my relationship with Jim Beam.)

Fiona told me she loved Ben. That she was sorry she had been the "other woman" but she really didn't know about me at first, and by the time she did she loved him and it didn't matter how she had him. I recognized that feeling so well, recognized it from that night at the bar on Front Street when Ben and I first met, when we stood in the snow and kissed for the first time. Ben was indeed lovable and I couldn't very well blame her for falling for it. Besides, the warm, fuzzy feeling that was developing in my body as a result of the whisky was preventing me from having ill will towards anyone. It was also having the surprising effect of making her more attractive with each passing moment.

Fiona was so beautiful that she looked out of place in my tiny, cluttered apartment—as if she was a Christian Dior ad shoved into a comic book. Although I had managed to tidy things up a bit since my stint of Brian Wilson-esque madness, nothing in the room seemed to measure up to how impressive she was. She was so slender, delicate and pale, her features only further enhanced by the vibrant green of the tiny dress she was wearing. Her hair, which was an intense (and of course, natural) shade of tangerine, fell in almost perfect ringlets around her heart-shaped face and cascaded dramatically down her back. Her voice was delicate and sweet, and just as I remembered from the Shoppers Drug Mart the day I had first seen her, she was *considerate*. She touched my hand while we spoke and seemed to constantly check in with me to see how well I was accepting the knowledge of my former love's infidelity.

Yes, she had fucked my boyfriend, but I also felt some sympathy for her now that she was sure Ben had the wandering eye. She told me she had witnessed some covert cell phone conversations and found phone numbers written on the inside of matchbooks. Because she already knew that Ben had a propensity towards infidelity she was sure he was bedding someone on the side. This was something I simply couldn't understand given that she looked like a supermodel and was, surprisingly enough, actually pretty fun to hang out with.

Five drinks in Fiona said, "You know, Marnie, you're really pretty."

I waited for the *but*. I waited intently for her to tell me what I could do to improve myself. I waited for the make-up instructions or hair styling tips. I waited for her to tell me to use pore-minimizing cleanser or to wear black because it was "slimming." I wouldn't have resented it—I figured Fiona would have fantastic advice to give, given she had managed to steal my boyfriend and that she was the most attractive woman I had ever seen.

But none of it ever came. According to Fiona, I was just pretty. Full stop.

"Thanks, Fiona." At this point I was drinking directly from the bottle and passing it to her after each mouthful.

"I can really see why Ben fell in love with you," she added, tossing her head back and taking a dramatic swig. Her head tilted back like that really emphasized how impossibly long—*swanlike*—her neck was.

"Can I ask you something, Fiona?"

"Shoot." Fiona was clearly drunk now. And somehow, we were friends.

"Why did *you* fall in love with Ben?" The question really had been on my mind since she arrived. What did this beautiful girl see in a boy who clearly didn't deserve her?

"You know what, Marnie? I have no fucking idea."

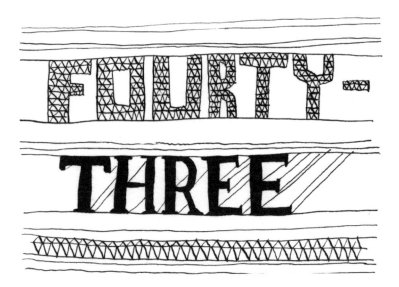

FOURTY-THREE

Reasons why I accidentally fell in love with Ben in the first place:

1–His unflinching loyalty to his less than perfect friends. Friends who came over and trashed his place during parties. Friends who left him waiting at gigs after forgetting they'd made plans with him.

2–The fact that he paid a DJ to play a song I wanted to hear (Ramble On by Led Zeppelin) even though he disliked Led Zeppelin and was otherwise very vocal about it.
3–While he did have a tendency towards irresponsibility, Ben had patience, loyalty and tolerance in amounts I'd never witnessed.
4–When the clinic called to confirm the appointment, Ben let me know that "everything is going to be okay."
5–My heart was already long broken and I assumed it wasn't possible for him to break it any more.

FOURTY-FOUR

And then Fiona was kissing me.

We were discussing some of Ben's finer characteristics and all of a sudden she abruptly reached across the table and grabbed me. While doing so she knocked her whisky glass onto the floor. It abruptly smashed all over the linoleum, but we just kept kissing. There was a childish awkwardness to it that surprised me. I had already spent much of the time that Fiona was across the

kitchen table from me fantasizing about how smooth she must be with members of the opposite sex—essentially that she was my sexual polar opposite. But hers was a groping gracelessness I revelled in, a clumsy hunger that I hadn't experienced in a while. That I hadn't experienced since Ben.

I was kissing Ben's girlfriend.

Ben's drunk girlfriend.

Ben's girlfriend that I had gotten drunk.

And Ben's drunk girlfriend was a fantastic kisser.

Suddenly I was eleven years old, learning how to kiss boys again.

Fiona pulled back for a moment to look at me, smoothing my hair out of my face and cupping my chin in her hands. I looked away quickly, her intense gaze suddenly making me uncomfortable.

"It's okay, Marnie," she said. "There's nothing wrong with kissing."

FOURTY-FIVE

The loneliness that Ben left behind him was like a tomb. It was so large and consuming I had to climb inside it, live inside it, hide inside it.

Ben conveniently left behind a particular brand of mistrust that made it impossible to meet anyone new or to even manage to carry on a conversation with a sales clerk at a shoe store. It certainly made grocery shopping intolerable. When people spoke to me I retreated, ran away as politely and as fast as I could to avoid any connection. When I would venture outside I'd hide behind dark sunglasses like I was an incognito movie star, concealing my face with scarves pulled up to my nose and hats pulled down over my eyebrows.

Maybe I didn't want to see or speak with anyone because I didn't want to explain how miserable I was that the only person I felt had understood me had left me because he couldn't stand me anymore.

FOURTY-SIX

More than a dozen little homeopathic viles in my medicine cabi-
net. Each one promising the madness that overcame me would
cease.

*Cherry Plum promised to assuage a fear of reason giving way, of
my own capacity to do fearful and dreaded things.*
*Clematis would relieve my dreaminess and drowsiness, revive
my interest in life and reduce my unhappiness with my present
circumstances.*

Gorse was for great hopelessness, when I had given up belief that anything more could be done for me.

Heather would prevent me from seeking the companionship of anyone who might be available.

Holly would relieve my thoughts of jealousy, envy, revenge, and suspicion.

Pine would prevent me from blaming myself.

Star of Bethlehem would help my great distress and unhappiness.

Sweet Chestnut for when it seemed there was nothing but destruction and annihilation left to face.

And White Chestnut was to keep away the thoughts, ideas, and arguments I didn't desire, the ones that circled round and round, causing endless anxiety.

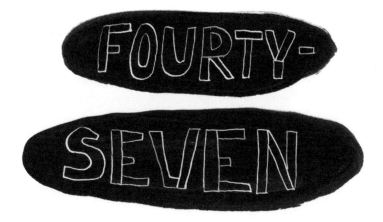

FOURTY-SEVEN

"Let's steal his dog," Fiona said.

We had finally stopped kissing and we were now lying on our backs beside each other, sharing our third Belmont Mild from the wooden box under my bed. They were a bit stale, given that I had pretended to quit for the third time and was only occasionally covertly smoking, but with the amount of whisky that was being passed around neither of us cared.

At this point Fiona and I had been drinking for about four hours. Somehow Fiona's dress had managed to come off, something that certainly had nothing to do with me. It actually didn't surprise me at all when she suddenly stood up from the kitchen table and pulled it up and over her head. She seemed like the type of girl who took off her clothes whenever she could.

Once she was successfully de-clothed, Fiona lay down on the floor next to the cat and began to scratch the animal's eager brow. Her emerald green dress was now hanging haphazardly off of my living room's only armchair, but her extravagant animal-print shoes were still on her feet. Lying there, in her simple black cotton underwear and bra, she continued to clash dramatically with her surroundings, namely me. She arched her back dramatically and exhaled a cloud of smoke above her while I watched sheepishly. Her partial nudity made me pull up my knee socks and pull on a cardigan.

"You want to steal Bill?" I replied, trying desperately not to look directly at any exposed portions of her incredibly pale skin, something that was a challenge given that she was only a few feet from me.

She passed me the cigarette and rolled over onto her stomach. "Yah. Bill. I fucking love that dog. Ben doesn't deserve that dog." She took another swig of whisky and snatched the cigarette back from me without giving me a chance to take a drag.

Over the past few hours we had managed a clumsy kissing and groping session and established that Ben was a complete and total asshole. Although we hadn't actually figured out who it was that he had been cheating on Fiona with, with our drunken logic and need to justify the fact that we had sucked face, we were completely certain he had been cheating on her with someone.

"How are we going to steal a dog?" I asked while sitting up, genuinely intrigued by the idea.

"I still have a key. We'll just go and get him. It won't even be like stealing. It'll be like saving."

I pondered the simplicity of this plan for a moment. Fiona was right in thinking that Ben needed to be punished, and if I tried hard enough I could develop a rationale that involved the injustice of such a beautiful dog staying in the possession of a deceitful philanderer. The rationale was the same one that made kissing her acceptable.

"You'll have to put your dress back on."

FOURTY-EIGHT

Rather pathetically, I remembered Ben's schedule well enough to know that he wasn't home when Fiona suggested we go steal his dog. Thursday nights meant band practice at 7 p.m., so the house in Parkdale was completely empty when Fiona and I stumbled out of a cab and up Ben's driveway. I remembered that Bill was always baby-gated off in the mudroom at the back of the house when the boys went out, and we crept towards him as quietly as possible for two drunk girls endeavoring to steal a 120-pound Neapolitan mastiff. To coax Bill out of his room and into our care Fiona grabbed some milk bones from a bag under the sink. I felt wounded by the fact that she knew her way around Ben's place in the same way I once did. Again, I tried not to think about how her subject of academic study translated into Ben's messy bedroom.

I had certainly warmed up to Fiona, but the idea that she had introduced Ben to bondage was simply too much to handle.

Fiona looked slightly absurd teetering around on her sexy shoes while clutching a handful of dog bones, and they proved unnecessary when we finally encountered Bill at the back of the house. While I removed the gate he was entirely thrilled to see us, twirling excitedly in circles, jumping up and thrusting his massive weight at us to the point where Fiona was knocked off of her feet. She laughed loudly at this and I urged her to shut up, as if I had some fear that we would be caught for breaking, entering and dog-stealing. Bill climbed on top of her and began licking her face lovingly, only increasing the volume of her fit of giggles.

I grabbed Bill's beloved stuffed Velveteen Rabbit from his dog bed with one hand and pulled Fiona to her feet with the other. I knew Ben and his roommates wouldn't likely be home before midnight, but being inside his house and all of the memories that came rushing back with that was giving me a case of hives.

"C'mon Fiona, let's go," I said, grabbing Bill by his red-leather spiked collar and scratching aggressively at my chest with my other hand. Bill had his stuffed bunny in his mouth and was shaking it around violently while I attempted to lead him to the front door.

"Um, Marnie? How are... where are we taking this dog?"

Obviously this was a part of our diabolic, ingenious plan we hadn't yet considered. The whisky was wearing off and I suddenly realized Ben's new girlfriend and I were stealing a dog, his dog. It felt too late to retreat from the plan, so I grabbed Bill's leash from the front hall table and pulled him out the door and down the street. I heard Fiona locking the door behind me and then the rapid clicking of her heels as she ran after us.

"I'm taking this dog home," I told her without looking behind me. "You're welcome to come with me if you like."

But Fiona really didn't look like she was going anywhere but to bed. She was bent over at the waist, vomiting into the household's curbside garbage can.

FOURTY-NINE

By the time I got back to my place my dignity and my whisky buzz were pretty much gone—all that remained was the broken glass on my kitchen floor and a pounding headache.

I had managed to get Fiona home in what turned out to be the most absurd cab ride I'd ever taken. In the back seat both her and the dog had their heads out the windows on either side of me as we travelled along Queen Street West towards Fiona's place in Kensington Market. When we finally arrived at her apartment (which of course was above a vintage clothing store) she could barely get inside. I had to ask the cab driver to watch Bill while I helped her get her key in the lock. It was pretty fair to say that he was terrified of the hundred and twenty pounds of dog in the back of his cab, but agreed to transport us anyway, tempted by the almost twenty dollar fare from Parkdale to her place.

Fiona had actually tried to kiss me again before I managed to shove her inside her front door.

Olive was certainly not pleased that I brought Bill home with me. As soon as he made his appearance in my living room and collapsed dramatically on my couch she was hissing, spitting and then quickly retreating to her favourite hiding spot under the bed. Bill all but completely ignored her, content to alternate between sleep and chewing on one of my black Converse all-stars while I figured out what I was going to do with a massive dog in my tiny apartment.

It wouldn't be long before Ben figured out where Bill was—I knew when he discovered his dog gone from a locked house he'd accuse the only other person who had a key, and that person would rat me out within moments. I didn't imagine that Fiona, while sober, was still my loyal partner in crime and new best friend, and the fact that she'd blab was probably why I didn't feel guilty that I had stolen Bill.

Actually, I didn't feel guilty at all that Bill was now passed out on his back on my couch. I had a free pass to delinquent behaviour given that I had just hours before found out that Ben had been cheating on me with Fiona for two months.

All that felt beside the point now. While the details certainly seemed to justify the theft, they didn't have the capacity to hurt me anymore.

Nothing had the capacity to hurt me any more.

I felt free from it all.

Dogs sleep approximately eighteen hours a day.

A dog will tend to circle before lying down to sleep—this is what he would do in the wild, where he would trample down vegetation to create a bed, typically in longer grass where his presence would be concealed.

If it's cold, a dog will curl up in a ball to conserve body heat.

It's common for an adult dog to lie on his side while he's

sleeping, and start moving his legs as if he were running. The eyelids and whiskers may twitch at this stage, which is usually a sign of what we humans call "deep sleep."

Dogs generally spend most of their time sleeping lightly. Many dogs don't sleep deeply because they understand that they need to take the responsibility of watching over their pack.

Because of this, dogs instinctively wake when there is an increased amount of activity around them.

FIFTY-ONE

I still didn't have a phone, so the only thing left to do was to wait for Ben to come and get his dog. I switched off the television, which had been on continuously for months now, and lay down on my bed. I was still in my parka, and I thought about how soon it would be too heavy to wear in the spring thaw.

As I began to float off to sleep, thanks to my failing whisky haze, Bill dismounted the couch and meandered the short distance to the bed. He soon found his old spot in the angles made by my knees, rotating in a few circles until he was finally satisfied, and collapsing with a sigh, snug up against the backs of my thighs. Within moments he was snoring.

Together Bill and I drifted off, into a state of half asleep and half awake, watching out for each other while chasing things in dreams, killing time before it was time to go.

EPILOGUE

I gave notice on my apartment at the end of May. I called my landlord and let him know that I needed something bigger and he let me know he had a vacant two bedroom in another building he managed down the street.

I wasn't exactly sure what I was going to do with my bigger place (or how I was going to pay for it, for that matter) but after everything, I was sure I needed to space to stretch out. I was also pretty sure I wanted someone in the next room to remind me what I looked like. I put my ad for a roommate on Craigslist right away.

Maybe I'd get a dog.

One day I was packing boxes, the door to my apartment propped open so I could make frequent trips to the dumpster to purge all the many relics I'd managed to collect while in hiding, and Neil appeared in my doorway.

"You're leaving?" he asked without saying hello. His face revealed genuine disappointment.

"Yup. Moving down the street. I have all these books to return to you," I said, motioning toward a box with his name scrawled on it in red marker.

"I see you still have Bill."

Bill was on the couch, reclining on his back with his tongue hanging out of his mouth. He hadn't even bothered to get up when Neil arrived. Olive was curled in a tight little ball, snug up against him.

"Yah, I'm watching the dog for a few weeks while Ben's on tour with his band."

"It's nice that the two of you can still be friends," he said, while leaning down to pick up his box of borrowed books.

Friends was a real stretch. Reality was that I loved Bill enough to fake friendship with Ben for visitation rights. The kidnapping incident had, surprisingly, resulted in custody every second weekend and first dibs on dogsitting while Ben and his band mates were out of town. It also meant I was able to see Fiona on occasion, who was growing on me.

"You look really well, Marnie."

"The books must be helping."

When Panic Attacks: Change your Mind, Change Your Life
Fear: Why you shouldn't be afraid of it
How Our Parents' Apathy Makes Us Fragile
And my personal favourite,
The Healing Power of Rover

I lied. I hadn't actually read any of the books. What was really helping was the fact that being alone didn't bother me so much any more. I wasn't sure why, but a cloud had lifted that inspired me to throw away all of the things I was saving in search of disaster.

Maybe it was kissing Fiona at my kitchen table, but more likely it was seeing her vomit in a garbage can. An image like that can prove to be a powerful one.

Maybe it was seeing Ben at my front door, ready to collect his stolen dog, and realizing that I didn't miss him as helplessly as I thought I did. Maybe it was the selfish satisfaction in discovering that maybe he missed me a little more than I missed him. That he still thought I was beautiful. That he regretted ditching me for a girl he fucked in a filthy bathroom stall.

It didn't matter. Surrounded by moving boxes and garbage bags, I knew that I was no longer suspended between a past of standing on tabletops drinking shooters and a future of settling; I was something else entirely.

I was finally seeing myself.

Hello, my name is Marnie. I've been unbroken.

WHAT YOU NEED TO HANG WALLPAPER BY YOURSELF:

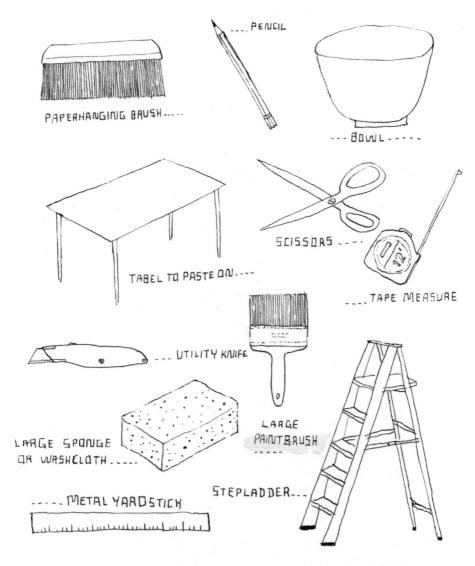

PENCIL

PAPERHANGING BRUSH.....

---BOWL-----

TABEL TO PASTE ON----

SCISSORS -----

.... TAPE MEASURE

--- UTILITY KNIFE

LARGE PAINTBRUSH

LARGE SPONGE OR WASHCLOTH.....

STEPLADDER...

-----METAL YARDSTICK

ARE YOU READY TO WALLPAPER NOW?

Acknowledgements

Stacey May Fowles

First and foremost thanks go to Marlena Zuber for being the most fantastic partner in crime a writer could ever ask for. Thanks to Robbie MacGregor, Nic Boshart and Megan Fildes at Invisible Publishing for all of their faith, talent and support. Thanks to my indispensable editor Ari Berger for making everything happen and making it happen better than I ever could alone.

Thanks to the Canada Council for the Arts, the Ontario Arts Council and the City of Toronto through the Toronto Arts Council for their financial support.

Thanks to the participants at Nightwood Theatre's Write From The Hip! program for seeing this book through to the stage. Thanks to Alissa York and Diaspora Dialogues for their commitment to the development of emerging voices. Thanks to Michael Redhill for being my literary mentor, friend and occasional much-needed kick in the pants.

Thanks to Megan Griffith-Greene for sharing her table, her stories, and her green beans with me. I am privileged to be your high-maintenance girlfriend. Thanks to the inspiring staff at *Shameless Magazine* for sharing their insight, wit and wisdom.

As always, thanks to my parents and my chosen family for loving and supporting me even in my darkest days and most neurotic moments. And finally, thank you to my beautiful, patient and tolerant husband, Spencer, without whom I would never have ridden the subway again. Our love is certainly "for reals".

Acknowledgements

Marlena Zuber

I am indebted to Stacey May Fowles for inviting me along for the adventure. Putting pictures to your words has been an honour. Thank you to Robbie MacGregor and Megan Fildes at Invisible Publishing for your support, guidance and confidence. Thank you also to Mom, Dad, Justin, Todd, Laurel, Steph, Leah, Heather, Paul, Mary-Jo, Nic, Sally, Jesse, James, the Creative Works Studio gang, Margaux, the Tomboyfriends and Zigby for very many nice reasons.

Stacey May Fowles's writing has appeared in various online and print magazines, including *Kiss Machine*, the *Absinthe Literary Review*, *Fireweed*, and *subTERRAIN*. Her work has been widely anthologized in books including *Nobody Passes: Rejecting The Rules of Gender and Conformity, First Person Queer, Yes Means Yes*, and *I.V. Lounge Nights*. Her first novel, *Be Good*, was published by Tightrope Books in 2007. Fowles recently adapted *Fear of Fighting* into a stage play as part of Nightwood Theatre's Write From The Hip! program for emerging female playwrights. She currently lives in Toronto where she is the publisher of *Shameless Magazine*.

Marlena Zuber is a freelance illustrator and artist. She graduated from the Ontario College of Art and Design and her illustrations have appeared in various publications including the *Washington Post*, the *Boston Globe*, the *Chicago Tribune, BUST Magazine* and *Print Magazine*.

Invisible Publishing is committed to working with writers who might not ordinarily be published and distributed commercially. We work exclusively with emerging and under-published authors to produce entertaining, affordable, books.

We believe that books are meant to be enjoyed by everyone and that sharing our stories is important. In an effort to ensure that books never become a luxury, we do all that we can to make our books more accessible.

We are collectively organized and our production processes are transparent. At Invisible, publishers and authors recognize a commitment to one another, and to the development of communities which can sustain and encourage storytellers.

If you'd like to know more please get in touch.
info@invisiblepublishing.com

Invisible Publishing
Halifax & Montréal